“Maybe together we can find a way for you to stop running.”

Sky snorted in contempt. “If it was that easy, don’t you think I’d have figured it out for myself by now? What makes you think that you can help me?”

“I’m stubborn and refuse to give up until I solve whatever mystery I’m working on. Give me a chance. Let me help you live a normal life, to not look over your shoulder everywhere you go. Don’t you want to interact with people, talk to them, have them listen to you, without worrying that they might recognize you and put you in danger because of whoever’s after you?”

She blinked. “How did you know?”

“That you feel isolated? That you long for normal human contact?”

She slowly nodded.

“How could you not? You’ve been living in fear for a long time. Maybe we can end that. All you have to do is trust me.”

A single tear slid down her face and she quickly wiped it away. “I don’t even know you. How can you expect me to trust you?”

SHROUDED IN THE SMOKIES

LENA DIAZ

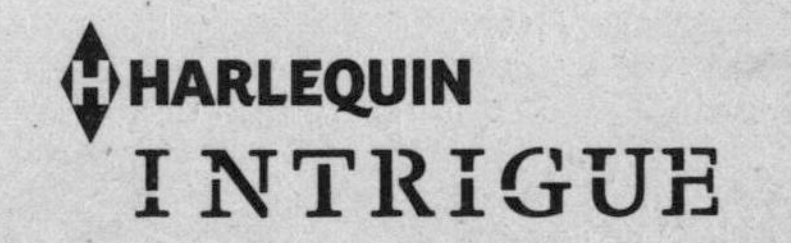

This story is dedicated to my recently passed beloved mother and mother-in-law, Letha and Marie. Every day without them is a struggle. Grief is a dagger in my heart. Life is short and unpredictable. Love, laugh, be kind. Say the things you need to say while you still can. No regrets.

HARLEQUIN®
INTRIGUE™

ISBN-13: 978-1-335-59104-3

Shrouded in the Smokies

For questions and comments about the quality of this book, please contact us at CustomerService@Harlequin.com.

Harlequin Enterprises ULC
22 Adelaide St. West, 41st Floor
Toronto, Ontario M5H 4E3, Canada
www.Harlequin.com

Printed in U.S.A.

Lena Diaz was born in Kentucky and has also lived in California, Louisiana and Florida, where she now resides with her husband and two children. Before becoming a romantic suspense author, she was a computer programmer. A Romance Writers of America Golden Heart® Award finalist, she has also won the prestigious Daphne du Maurier Award for Excellence in Mystery/Suspense. To get the latest news about Lena, please visit her website, lenadiaz.com.

Books by Lena Diaz

Harlequin Intrigue

A Tennessee Cold Case Story

Murder on Prescott Mountain
Serial Slayer Cold Case
Shrouded in the Smokies

The Justice Seekers

Cowboy Under Fire
Agent Under Siege
Killer Conspiracy
Deadly Double-Cross

The Mighty McKenzies

Smoky Mountains Ranger
Smokies Special Agent
Conflicting Evidence
Undercover Rebel

Tennessee SWAT

Mountain Witness
Secret Stalker
Stranded with the Detective
SWAT Standoff

Visit the Author Profile page at Harlequin.com.

CAST OF CHARACTERS

Adam Trent—Investigator for the civilian cold case company Unfinished Business. He's determined to solve the mystery of who's trying to kill Skylar and why.

Skylar Montgomery—This former nurse faked her death to escape an enemy hiding in the shadows. Now she's running for her life. Her only hope at a future is to work with Trent to solve the complicated mystery of her past.

Abby Montgomery—The secrets that Skylar's mother took to her grave may be the reason that someone is trying to kill her daughter.

Ryan Montgomery—Skylar's father lived a nomad's life, moving his family every few years and giving them aliases. For Skylar to live a normal life without fear, Trent will have to determine why Ryan was running.

Martha Lancaster—Matriarch of the Lancaster family, her good intentions may end up destroying everyone she loves.

Richard Lancaster—Martha's son runs a multimillion-dollar horse-breeding empire. But it may be a front for a dangerous criminal enterprise.

Scott Lancaster—Martha's youngest son lives in his brother's shadow as he struggles to create his own legacy.

Chapter One

The Smoky Mountains above Gatlinburg, Tennessee, were Skylar's prison. Fear was the lock that kept her there, that wouldn't let her call out to the small group of hikers as they passed her hiding place a few feet from the trail. Her throat tightened with longing. She wanted to step around the bushes, to shout, to beg them to turn around.

See me. Hear me. Talk to me.

But, like all the times before, she didn't. She couldn't. If they saw her, recognized her, then all the hiding, the running, the years of isolation would be for nothing.

Instead, she picked up her towel and bar of soap, and turned away from the now-empty trail. She trudged through the woods to the creek where she'd planned to bathe before the distant laughter had been too compelling to resist. But even the beautiful lavender-colored wildflowers pushing up through the soil to welcome spring couldn't lighten her mood.

What would it be like to be that carefree? To laugh without worrying about being heard? To have meaningful conversations instead of a mumbled thank you, head bent, as she bought supplies in some random town before escaping back to wherever she was hiding that particular week.

Skylar dropped to her knees, the moss-covered ground cool against her bare legs. Normally, the beauty of the gurgling water and the leafy hemlocks marching up and down the Tennessee Smoky Mountain foothills would have had her smiling. But it seemed that nothing could ease her troubled thoughts today.

Almost five years of running, hiding, living like a hermit had taken its toll. She was tired, bone-numbingly exhausted from being on high alert all the time. What was the point of fighting anymore? Maybe she should quit, give up, surrender to what was likely inevitable anyway.

One more day, Sky. Just one more. You can quit tomorrow.

That's what her Army Ranger father would have told her, what he *had* told her, until the words were branded into her soul. Like when she'd complained as a teenager during their pre-dawn runs, begging him to let her stop to catch her breath.

One more mile, Sky. Just one more. You can quit tomorrow.

Or when her arms felt like jelly and she wanted to get out of the pool.

Daddy, please. I don't want to swim anymore. Can't I go to the mall with my friends instead?

One more lap, Sky. Just one more. You can do it, sweetie. Dig deep. Do it for Daddy.

And she had. Rather than disappoint him, she'd run one more mile, swam one more lap, fired at the target over and over until her pattern was almost as tight and accurate as her father's.

But the desire to please him wasn't always enough. Her body would sometimes give out and she'd drop from exhaustion. Oddly, those were the good times, the best of times. Because that's when her daddy would scoop her up in his strong arms, his brow furrowed with worry and regret as he apologized for pushing her so hard.

He'd spoil her with a decadent dessert. They'd play video games for hours, even though he hated them. He'd let her stay up late watching her favorite TV shows even if it was a school night, all the while vowing he wouldn't push her quite so hard the next time.

But he did. He always did.

Even when she'd started her nursing studies at the University of San Diego, he'd show up most mornings to work out with her or go for a run before the sun came up. He'd never stopped their routine, encouraging her to keep going, telling her she could quit tomorrow. But of course, the catch was that tomorrow never came. It was always a day away. Quitting was never really an option.

Even after he'd been tragically killed by a drunk driver when she was halfway through her sophomore year, she'd continued to push herself the same way that he had. Hoping to find some long-lost relatives on her mother's side of the family, she'd transferred to UTC in Chattanooga. She'd never discovered any relatives. But she'd settled into her new life and continued her father's training tradition. It was an ingrained habit. And it felt like a betrayal to even think about stopping.

She'd also matured enough by then to at least partly

understand her father's obsession. He'd been driven by grief over the loss of her mother when Skylar was a little girl. He didn't want to lose Skylar too. And since he couldn't protect her from sickness, like the cancer that had taken her mom, he'd protected her the only way he knew how—by making sure she could outrun or outfight anyone who tried to hurt her.

Years later, when she'd walked out of the hospice center where she volunteered on weekends and saw a suspicious-acting man watching her from across the street, muscle memory had kicked in. She'd dropped to the ground and rolled to safety seconds before bullets whistled past her, so close she'd swear she could feel their heat.

That night, she'd whispered prayers asking God to tell her daddy she loved him and to let him know that all those lessons had paid off. If it wasn't for the grueling training he'd put her through, treating her like one of his Special Forces Rangers, she'd never have survived that day. And she certainly wouldn't have survived the next attempt on her life, or the next, or the ensuing handful of years on the run.

And if she didn't leave here, soon, she'd throw away all that hard work, all the faith her father had put in her.

She'd been lulled into a false sense of security by this place, these lush green mountains, so beautiful and peaceful. And she'd stayed longer than she should have, longer than she'd ever stayed in one place before. She should have left weeks ago.

Every day she remained increased the risk that someone would recognize her during one of her infrequent but necessary trips into Gatlinburg for supplies. They could have told someone, who told someone else, until word got back to the person, or people, who wanted her dead. It was time to wash, pack up her meager belongings and find another place to live for a while.

She took her pistol out of the pocket of her shorts and set it on the bank, not wanting to risk it falling into the swiftly moving water. Down by the creek, she carefully pulled her treasured necklace off. The thick gold chain sparkled in the sunlight filtering through the trees overhead, making her smile.

Her friends had been given cars, or luggage, or wads of cash at their high school graduations. To celebrate Skylar's diploma, her father had given her a chunky gold chain with a gleaming gold compass suspended from it. The twinge of disappointment she'd felt when he handed it to her had evaporated when she'd read the inscription on the back.

One more, Skylar. Just one more. You can quit tomorrow.

That saying was a better send-off into her future than any commencement speech. It was a reminder that as long as she worked hard, she could do anything, go in any direction she wanted. More importantly, it was a reminder of his love for her.

She carefully set it aside. As she started to pull the shirt over her head, a whisper of sound had her whirling around. A tall, thin man stood less than twenty feet away.

"Finally found you." His voice was harsh, gritty.

A gray, hooded sweatshirt concealed his features. But even if it hadn't, the sun was behind him, casting his face into shadow. Not that she cared. It was the pistol in his hand that had her attention. It was a shiny new-looking Heckler & Koch HK45 semi-automatic. The same kind of gun her father had favored. Expensive. Powerful. Deadly. Particularly since the muzzle was pointed directly at her chest.

Was this the man who'd forced her to flee Chattanooga all those years ago? Or had her nemesis sent yet another one of his minions to try to kill her?

"Who are you? What do you want?" She stalled for time as she glanced up the bank to where she'd left her gun. Too far from her. Too close to the gunman. "I can't see your face, so I can't identify you to the authorities. Just leave, go. I promise I won't tell anyone you were here."

He laughed. "No way. I got paid to do this, lady. Got paid real good. And I'm gettin' more when this is done."

"Who hired you?" Those trees, to her right. They'd provide cover. But could she make it to them without getting shot?

"I didn't ask the dude's name." He straightened his arm, squinting as he awkwardly lined up the pistol's sights, seemingly unfamiliar with the weapon. Had the man who'd hired him given him the gun?

"I'll pay you more than he did." She braced her feet, getting ready. "I'll double whatever he paid you if you let me go. I've got plenty of money."

He chuckled, but the pistol didn't waver. "Good to know. After I kill you, I'll take that money."

She dove to the side.

Bam! Bam!

The second her feet hit the ground, she rolled and came up running.

His shout of rage echoed through the trees as he took off in pursuit.

Chapter Two

Trent stopped mid-stride, clutching the phone to his ear as he turned, scanning the forest on either side of the trail.

"What the heck?" Callum's voice demanded over the phone. "Was that gunfire?"

"That'd be my guess."

Bam! Bam!

Trent whirled around, pinpointing the direction of the shots. They'd come from the west. He hopped over the logs forming a short wall beside the hiking path and jogged toward the trees.

"Trent? What's going on?"

"What's going on is that my rare Monday off from work to take advantage of the gorgeous spring weather isn't going at all the way I'd hoped."

"Trent—"

"Call 911, Callum. Get the park rangers out here, the law enforcement kind, not the tour guides. Some idiot's firing a gun in our national park and I, for one, don't appreciate him shooting so close to the trail."

"If you're asking *me* to call 911, what the heck are *you* doing?"

"I'm going to stop the idiot, of course, before he hurts someone."

Bam!

He automatically ducked, then took off in the direction of the latest shot.

"Trent. For the love of… Do you even have your gun with you?"

"It's a national park, Callum. That would be illegal."

"Please tell me you're kidding."

"Afraid not."

Callum swore. "Text me your GPS coordinates. I'll pass them to another team member to call 911 and coordinate with the Rangers so I can stay on the line with you." After Trent paused to provide him the information, Callum said, "All right. Give me a sec."

Trent crouched behind some trees as he scanned his surroundings. As near as he could figure, the shots had come from this vicinity. But he didn't see anyone.

Callum came back on the line. "Okay, stay where you are. Wait for the rangers. Ivy's talking with them right now. They're not too far away. Your buddy, Ranger Adam McKenzie, is leading them. He's training some new recruits at the bottom of the mountain near the entrance to the trail you're on, says they can be there in under eight minutes."

"Tell McKenzie that's about seven minutes too late. He needs to double-time it up here, preferably before I become another sad statistic."

"Stop joking, Trent."

"You don't hear me laughing, do you?"

Another shot echoed through the trees to his left. A woman cried out, just for a second and abruptly stopped, as if she hadn't meant to make any noise, or someone had cut her off mid-shout. Either way, things had just gotten way more serious with a potential victim involved. He swore and took off again.

"Trent! Whatever you're doing, stop. I mean it, man. Wait for the guys who get paid to do this stuff. You're not a cop anymore and you aren't armed. You get that, right? They have your GPS coordinates. Just wait—"

"No can do, buddy. This isn't some fool out for target practice. I heard a woman cry out, obviously in trouble." He left the line open so Callum could track him but shoved the phone into his pants pocket. He crept deeper into the brush, then stopped.

There, twenty yards ahead to the left, his right profile turned to Trent, was presumably the man who'd been shooting. He was partially hidden by a huge pine tree. Unfortunately, a hoodie and the gloom of the forest concealed most of his features. About all Trent could be sure of was that the guy was white. Or maybe Latino. Or, dang it, Trent couldn't be sure of anything, except that there was a pistol in the guy's hand. It was slowly moving back and forth, as if he was searching for someone.

Trent figured it was a safe bet the gunman's target was the woman to Trent's right. From his vantage point, he could see her left profile, barely. She was peering through some branches on a fallen log, her gaze riveted on the man pointing the gun in her direction. He must not have seen her yet, or he'd be shooting instead of scanning the forest with his pistol as if it was a divining rod. But it was only a matter of time before he'd find her. She needed a better place to hide.

The slope of the mountain on her far side and behind her would be too steep to climb quickly. And the sparse brush and trees on that slope would give the shooter a perfect view of his prey. Her only real choice was the relatively flat, thick forest around Trent. But to reach him, she'd have to get past a bald spot devoid of bushes and trees.

She was trapped.

Two more shots boomed. The woman didn't move. The shooter did. His pea-sized brain must have finally figured out that if he'd pursued her this far, there was only one place to hide—behind the massive fallen log where she was currently crouched.

Aiming his pistol at the log, he crept across the clearing.

Trent sorely regretted his decision not to break the law and bring a pistol on his early morning jaunt through the Smoky Mountains National Park. He blamed his poor decision on his former career as a police officer. That whole respect for the law thing could be a definite liability sometimes. Like now.

Hoodie-man was getting closer. Soon, he'd be able to see the woman.

Trent looked around, scrambling in the leaves and dirt for something to throw at the shooter. A broken branch. A rock. Anything heavy. One well-placed hit to his arm or head would be the distraction Trent needed to give the woman a chance to run, and Trent a chance to charge the gunman and tackle him, preferably without getting shot.

But there weren't any rocks or branches close by. There was nothing but leaves and a few flowers, or maybe weeds, scattered around. Brain-child over there *might* be distracted by someone throwing flowers into the air. But Trent wasn't willing to bet his life on it. He needed to come up with a Plan B, because Plan A involved making himself a target. Plan A pretty much sucked.

The gunman continued to advance. A few more steps and it would be over for the woman.

He let out a disgusted sigh. *Plan A, it was.*

Trent leaned around a tree, cupped his hands to his mouth and yelled the stupidest phrase that he and his brothers-in-blue had been forced by misguided policies to use for years. It was the equivalent of saying, *Here I am. Shoot me, please.* Except that it sounded instead like, "Police. Freeze!"

No surprise, the gunman whirled toward Trent, firing.

Trent ducked as bullets tore through the brush around him, pinging off bark and shredding leaves inches from the tree he was behind. The pounding of footsteps told him his ploy to distract the gunman had worked, a little too well. The jerk with the gun was running straight for Trent.

"Couldn't have picked a better day for a stupid hike," he muttered under his breath as he took off running, zigzagging through the forest, bullets strafing the ground far too close to him.

A few minutes later, he was in the same situation that the woman had been. He was hunkered down behind a log with the gunman searching for him. He dug in his pocket for his phone.

"Callum," he whispered. "Any chance those rangers

are going for a speed record and are here already but I just don't see them?"

"ETA three minutes. What the heck is going on? Sounds like World War III out there."

"The good news is that I managed to save the woman. The bad news is there's no one here to save me."

"Don't be so sure about that," a feminine voice whispered behind him.

He jerked around. The petite brunette he'd seen earlier was crouched a few yards away. And this time, she was holding a gun.

"Stay down," she whispered.

"O…kay. What are you going to—"

She jerked upright and let loose with a volley of shots over his head.

Chapter Three

Trent swore and crouched closer to the ground.

Answering shots sounded from the clearing. The woman ducked behind a tree, then peered out from the other side and fired off a few more rounds.

The sound of someone crashing through the woods told Trent the gunman was running again, but this time he was running away.

"Slimy coward," the woman said through gritted teeth. She started to move past Trent, but he grabbed her and yanked her down right before another volley of shots pinged through the trees, inches from where she'd stood.

Her dark brown eyes widened in surprise as she looked at him. The forest went silent. No more shots. No more...anything. Even the birds had quit chirping.

Trent motioned to her to be quiet.

She gave him a *no kidding* look.

He grinned.

Her eyes widened in the universal *you're crazy* expression.

Maybe he was, because he was actually having fun.

They waited a full minute, before he slowly turned

and peered over the top of the log. When he didn't see any movement, and no more shots were fired, he ducked and motioned to her. They both scooted behind a nearby oak tree that provided better cover and allowed them to sit up.

She faced him, gun aimed at the ground with her finger on the frame instead of the trigger. Someone had trained her well. Interesting.

"I think he's gone now," Trent whispered.

"He'll be back. He's not about to throw away this chance."

"Chance at what?"

"To kill me, of course. You might have noticed he's been shooting at me."

"I noticed I was a target too. Crazy boyfriend? Jealous husband?"

She rolled her eyes. "I don't know who he is."

"Some random guy is chasing you through the Smokies, trying to kill you?"

"Something like that."

"Maybe he's a serial killer. Hopefully he's not of the Hannibal Lecter variety. I'm fresh out of Chianti."

She gave him the *something is seriously wrong with you look* and nodded toward the clearing. "Thanks for distracting him earlier. I was in real trouble. The one time I left my gun on the bank too far away to…" Her mouth compressed in a tight line. "Anyway, thanks."

"The one time? There've been other times people shot at you?"

"I didn't say that."

That wasn't much of a denial. "You've got your gun now. How did that happen?"

"I ran back for it when he went after you. It wasn't far."

"Glad you did. I'm pretty sure you saved my life."

Her mouth quirked, as if she wanted to smile, but wasn't sure how. "I guess we're even."

He held out his hand. "Adam Trent. Friends call me Trent. Given the circumstances, I figure you qualify."

She hesitated, warily eyeing his hand before shaking it. "Skylar…ah, Anderson."

He wondered at the hesitation before she'd told him her last name. "Skylar. Can't remember the last time I heard that name. It does have a familiar ring to it, though. Have we met? I mean, I know that sounds like I'm trying to hit on you, which would be really weird with everything that's happened. But, seriously, have we met?"

Her eyes widened, then she looked away. "I'm sure I would have remembered if we had."

Alarm bells were ringing in his mind. There was something so familiar about her, something flitting around in the fog of his memories, something that wouldn't quite come into focus.

Striking, deep brown eyes.

Delicate, oval face.

A surprising smattering of freckles across the bridge of her nose.

So. Dang. Familiar.

The hair, though, that didn't match whatever image his mind was conjuring. It was wavy, shoulder-length, a kind of reddish-brown. Maybe she'd changed the color and style since he'd seen her before. He had zero doubt that he *had* seen her. It was only a matter of time before he figured out when, or at least where.

He watched her eyes, her expression, while he carefully maintained a look of nonchalance as if he wasn't riddled with curiosity. Who was she? And why didn't she want him to know?

"I'm good with faces." He carefully weighed her reactions. "I'm sure it will come to me why yours seems so familiar. It always does."

Her eyes widened again. "Always?"

He nodded. "I'm a detective. Or, I was." He went in for the kill. "It helps that I have a photographic memory."

She swallowed. "You're a cop?"

The photographic memory hadn't shaken her. What had was hearing about his former career choice. Now *that* was interesting, and suspicious.

"*Was* a cop, Chattanooga PD. Now I'm a civilian here in Gatlinburg, an investigator helping law enforcement with cold cases all over Eastern Tennessee for a company called Unfinished Business. Heard of it?"

She slowly shook her head. "Can't say that I have." Her voice sounded strained, and she'd noticeably stiffened when he'd mentioned Chattanooga PD. Was she from Chattanooga?

"We're still fairly new. Been operating over a year now. Are you from Gatlinburg? Pigeon Forge?"

"Passing through." She peeked around the tree again. "I think he's gone. It's probably safe to—"

"I'd feel better if you waited."

"For what?"

"Not what. Who. The cavalry is on the way, park

rangers, the law-enforcement variety. Should be here any minute."

"You called the police?"

"My teammates, Ivy and Callum, did. I was on the phone with Callum when I first heard gunshots." Her face had gone alarmingly pale. "I'm getting the vibe that you're more worried about the cops than the gunman."

She stared at him. "You're kidding, right? That guy was trying to kill me."

"Which is why your reactions are confusing. You seem more afraid of the rangers coming, and the fact that I'm a former cop, than you did of your would-be murderer. Why is that?"

She shook her head, as if to deny the obvious. But before she said anything, a muted voice sounded behind her. There were flashes of movement as a group of people headed toward them through the thick brush.

"I'll bet that's my buddy, Ranger Adam McKenzie, leading the pack." He motioned to her gun. "You might want to put that away so they don't think you're the threat. Is that what you're worried about? That you broke the law by bringing a firearm into a federal park?"

She glanced at the gun. "I, ah, yes. I imagine there are stiff penalties for things like that." She shoved her pistol into her waistband and yanked her shirt down to cover it.

"You'll get some flack about it. But considering you saved my life, I think they'll be more intent on finding the guy who was shooting at us."

Obviously, she was lying. He'd bet his 401K that she knew exactly why that gunman had gone after her and she didn't want anyone in law enforcement to know about it.

He peered through the brush at the approaching rangers. Once McKenzie had her in an interrogation room, maybe he'd get some honest answers and share them with Trent.

"I'll make sure they know we're friendlies to put their trigger fingers at ease. Stay right behind me. Otherwise, they may mistake you for the bad guy and start shooting."

"O...okay."

They stood and headed through the woods toward the rangers. There were five of them, with McKenzie in front.

Trent called his name, announcing himself as he stepped out with his hands up. McKenzie smiled with obvious relief and quickly introduced his teammates.

"And this is Skylar Anderson," Trent said. "The woman who was being shot at." He turned around, motioning toward her.

Except, she wasn't there.

He swore and shook his head. He'd assumed his bogus warning about the rangers being trigger-happy would have kept her right behind him. But she must have realized they were professionals and wouldn't go off half-cocked. Either that, or she'd decided that keeping her secrets, and avoiding law enforcement, was worth the risk.

"We'll find her," McKenzie said. "Let's start with the shooter's description."

"Male, about six feet tall. In spite of the warm weather, he was wearing a gray sweatshirt with a hoodie. Doesn't take much to realize he wore that ensemble to disguise his features. He wore khaki pants, white sneakers. His face was too shadowed for me to catch more than a partial glimpse. From the way he moved, I got the impression he was young, late teens to early twenties. His hands were lightly tanned. I'm guessing he's Caucasian but he could be Latino or a light-skinned Black man."

"Weapons?"

"Only one that I saw, a pistol. I'm guessing 45 caliber."

"And the woman?"

"Caucasian, thirty-ish, about five foot two, athletic build, really thin, like she's not eating well enough. Can't weigh more than a buck five. Hair's shoulder length, reddish-brown. Dark brown eyes. She was wearing tan-colored shorts and a navy blue button-up shirt, brown hiking boots."

McKenzie barked orders to the men and women with him, directing one of them toward a cabin he said was close by, another to the west to try to cut off anyone's escape in that direction. The other two fanned out ahead of him and Trent as they headed into the brush so Trent could show McKenzie where the shooting had happened.

A short time later, it was clear that finding the shooter and Skylar was going to take a while. McKenzie radioed for backup and a crime scene team as he secured the clearing.

"We've got this, Trent. They're already closing the trailhead behind us and sending reinforcements. This whole section of the park will be crawling with rangers in a few minutes."

"Might as well warn you that she has a pistol too.

Looked to be 9 mil. But she used it only for self-defense when the shooter turned on us. She saved my life."

"You sure about that? You don't know her. Or do you?"

"Honestly, I'm not sure. She seemed familiar. I'd swear I've seen her somewhere."

"Then you'll figure it out with that amazing memory of yours. When you do, you'll call me?"

"As long as that goes both ways. You find her, let me know. I'm curious about her and what's going on. She's definitely hiding something."

McKenzie nodded. "You got it. Now get out of here before you muck up my crime scene." He smiled, letting Trent know he was teasing, then jogged toward one of the other rangers.

Trent left the clearing but hesitated when he heard the sound of gurgling water. There was a stream close by. Hadn't Skylar mentioned something about leaving her gun on the bank? Was that where she'd been when the shooter first went after her?

He glanced at McKenzie, but he was talking into his radio while looking at a map another ranger was holding up in front of him. Rather than interrupt them, Trent strode toward the sound of the water, figuring he could update McKenzie if he found anything.

A moment later he knew he was in the right spot. A towel and a bar of soap sat on the bank, close to a gurgling stream. Her camp must be close by, maybe the cabin McKenzie had mentioned. Seeing no evidentiary value in someone's bathing paraphernalia, he started back toward the trail. But something sparkling in the grass made him stop.

It was a gold chain. He scooped it up and realized it had a gold compass hanging off it. The compass was surprisingly heavy, much more solid than any he'd ever seen. Definitely built to last. Had the gunman dropped it? Or Skylar? He studied it a moment, then turned it over. On the back was an inscription: *One more, Sky. Just one more. You can quit tomorrow.*

Sky. Short for Skylar? Seemed like a safe bet. He glanced around, hoping to see one of the rangers so he could turn it in. But no one was in sight. Not wanting to leave the necklace to be lost or stepped on, he slid it into his shirt pocket. He'd call McKenzie later and exchange the necklace for an update on the investigation.

SKYLAR SWORE BENEATH her breath as she watched the former cop take off toward the trail with her compass necklace in his pocket. She should have searched for the necklace first, instead of sprinting to the cabin to throw her belongings into her backpack. But she wouldn't have gotten her backpack if she had. As soon as she'd made it into some tree cover, a ranger had emerged from the brush on the other side of the cabin and headed inside. The woods were crawling with law enforcement now. If she was going to catch up to, what was his name… Trent something? Or was it something Trent? Either way, she'd have to hurry to reach him before he got too far away.

She'd taken one step in the direction he'd gone when two more rangers showed up. Jerking back, she crouched low, praying they hadn't seen her. Luckily, they weren't looking her way. One of them was talking into a radio, something about a cabin. Her cabin, probably. Or, at least, what she'd commandeered as her cabin for the past month.

They passed within a few yards of her hiding place. She stayed as still and silent as possible. As soon as they were gone, she let out a shaky breath. Trent was long gone now. And things were getting way too dicey out here.

I'm sorry, Daddy. I'm so sorry.

She spared one last agonized glance toward where Trent, and her necklace, had disappeared, then whirled around and jogged deeper into the forest.

Chapter Four

The aroma of steak sizzling on a grill made Skylar's mouth water as she crept down the steeply sloped side yard to the left of Trent's cabin, perched on the edge of one of the Smoky Mountains. Her stomach decided to join the party, growling, reminding her that she hadn't eaten since this morning. But her empty stomach would have to wait. She hadn't spent half the day struggling to evade the rangers who were after her, then tracking Trent down, just to knock on his door and ask what's for dinner.

Especially since he'd told her that he never forgot a face.

She couldn't risk him seeing her again and possibly recognizing her, particularly since they'd both once lived in Chattanooga. And especially because he was a former cop. Today's close call emphasized it was time to find a new town to hide in. But she wasn't leaving without her necklace. That meant she had to perform some reconnaissance and find out where he'd put it, then figure out how to retrieve it without him seeing her.

Assuming he still had it.

There was always the possibility that he'd given it

to that relentless head ranger as evidence, the one he'd called McKenzie. That would mean it was lost to her forever. Her heart seemed to stutter in her chest at the thought of losing her last remaining physical tie to her father. She silently cursed McKenzie. Before today, she'd have never thought a ranger would be that determined to hunt her the way he had. It was more through luck than skill that she'd managed to evade him.

She'd stumbled into the path of a kindly old couple on a little two-lane road that wound around the outskirts of the Great Smoky Mountains National Park. They'd dropped her off at a hotel outside town after she'd lied about being a day hiker and said she had a room there. As soon as they'd left, she'd hiked to another hotel down the road and from there called a car service to pick her up.

A few more evasive maneuvers and another car service later had her ensconced in a cheap but thankfully clean motel, enjoying a hot shower for a change. Then she'd used their business center, equipped with a single computer, to search the Internet for Unfinished Business, the company that Trent had told her he worked for. Since their website gave backgrounds on their investigators, it was easy to find his picture and read his short bio. Adam, his first name was Adam. She'd forgotten that. From there, she'd searched the county's property tax appraiser's website to get his home address. Another short hike and here she was.

The tantalizing aroma lured her forward until she was at the back corner of the house. It was two stories—basement and main floor. There was no usable back yard, just a series of stilts anchoring the house into the side of the mountain, and a wood-lattice safety barrier to keep anyone from falling down that same mountain. Without some climbing gear and the willingness to risk plunging to her death, she wasn't going to access the basement from here and sneak into the house that way. But there was a flight of wooden stairs at the back left corner leading up to a deck off the main level above her. The outside light on that deck slanted through the boards, revealing a grill on the far side, and a man standing in front of it.

A hiss told her the steak had just been turned. Or maybe Trent had thrown some water on the fire to keep it from burning his dinner. That sound was quickly followed by the unmistakable deep tones of his voice. She tensed, clutching the straps of her backpack as she prepared to scramble up the side yard and into the woods if whoever he was speaking to ventured close enough to spot her. But there was no second voice. No other figure moving around on the deck. He must be on the phone. She held very still, straining to hear what he was saying.

"I'm not sure what to do with it," he said. "McKenzie was too busy to bother earlier. I suppose I can give him the necklace tomorrow."

Relief nearly made her light-headed. He hadn't given her necklace to the ranger. But he planned to. That meant she absolutely had to make her move tonight.

After he ended the call, some clinking sounds indicated he'd probably taken the steak off the grill and put it on a plate. Footsteps crossed the deck. A hinge creaked as he opened a door and went inside. A click told her the door had just closed. She tried to picture it. Not a sliding glass door, obviously, since she'd heard a hinge. It was probably a French door with little panes of glass, or maybe one solid glass sheet, so the mountain view wasn't obstructed. She was hoping for the kind with the little panes. If she couldn't jimmy the door open, she could break one of those panes without making too much noise.

Was he going to stay inside now to eat his dinner? From her vantage point below the deck, she could make out the outline of a small table and two chairs near the railing. But the mosquitoes were out in force right now. And although the sun had gone down and the cabin was high up in the mountain, it was still muggy out. On a night like this, she'd probably eat inside too, if given a choice. It was far preferable to fighting the bugs and the heat. Bug repellant was one of the main things she always kept in her backpack. But she preferred not to have to slather it on all the time.

Was he alone? There weren't any vehicles out front. But if a wife or girlfriend lived with him, their car could be in the garage where she assumed his was. She'd have to be careful, wait until he and anyone else inside went to bed. Because even though she had her gun, she didn't want to use it. Not on him, anyway. He'd helped her. And she didn't want to repay his kindness by shooting him.

Unless she absolutely had to.

She looked up at the sky to judge the time, as her father had taught her so long ago. Telling time by the stars was a complicated process involving finding the North Star, then the Big Dipper, making a calculation based on the current month. But she'd been doing it for so long it was automatic, easy. It was close to eight o'clock right now.

She figured most people would turn in by ten if they had to work the next day. Since today was Monday, she'd expect Trent to do the same. But if he was working this week, why was he in the park this morning? Maybe he was on vacation. If so, she had no way of predicting when he'd go to bed.

She sighed and resigned herself to several hours of waiting and watching. But staying out here in the open wasn't smart. The road out front wasn't heavily traveled, but it was curvy. Any car going down that road would likely see her in their headlights as they drove around the curves. No sense in risking being seen.

Hiding in the woods where she could keep watch on his cabin was the plan. Once all the lights were out and he'd had enough time to fall asleep, she'd return and make her move. It would take patience. And she was trusting that the lack of security system signs in the windows meant he didn't have one. Picking a lock was child's play. She'd done it many times, mostly to *borrow* a vacant cabin. But dealing with a burglar alarm wasn't in her repertoire. She settled her backpack more firmly on her shoulders and started up the slope.

Chapter Five

Trent watched from his hiding place as Skylar crept across the main room of his home. It was pitch dark, lit only by the LED lights from the media cabinet to the left of the stone fireplace. Hanging from one of the knobs on that cabinet was a gold compass on a chain, winking like a beacon amid the little green and red lights. It was a sparkly lure. And Skylar was the fish Trent hoped to catch.

The inscription on the back of the necklace told him it was likely sentimental. And it appeared to be an old piece that had been well-cared for. If anything was going to make her come out of hiding, it was the necklace. And it only made sense that if she realized someone had taken it, her first stop would probably be here, to see if he had it. Going to police headquarters or to the rangers to find it would be her last choice.

Her silence and stealth were impressive. It had only been by chance that he'd been on the deck to hear the snap of a twig beneath her shoes as she'd snuck through his side yard. He'd quickly pretended to be on the phone, talking about the necklace loud enough for her to overhear.

Now, as she crept through his main room, she was so quiet that he didn't hear her. If he hadn't already been crouched behind a recliner beside the fireplace, his eyes adjusted to the dark, he might not have seen her either. She was just a few feet away. If she'd looked down just then, she might have seen him. But she was too focused on her prize.

Her hand visibly shook as she reached up and swiped the necklace. She settled it over her head with a deep sigh, lifting her hair from beneath the chain to tuck the compass inside her shirt. The nearest LED light shined on her backpack, confirming Trent's suspicions. The item he'd noticed sticking out of the main flap was the butt of a pistol.

In one smooth motion, he stood, grabbed the gun, then rendered it safe.

Skylar jerked around with a startled gasp, searching the dark. But Trent had already zipped around the chair, moving like a wraith to the couch opposite the fireplace. Grabbing the remote control from the end table, he pressed a button. Lights flickered on overhead, chasing away the shadows.

Her mouth gaped open when she saw him. Brown eyes widened in alarm as her gaze dropped to her pistol in his right hand.

He shoved it in the waistband at his back and nodded in greeting. "Hello again, Skylar."

She took off like a startled fawn, sprinting toward the left side of the open concept room into the kitchen area, her backpack bouncing as she ran. He couldn't help feeling a twinge of empathy when she reached the set of French doors that opened onto the back deck.

Per his plan, he'd made it easy for her to pick the simple doorknob lock to get inside. Getting out, however, would challenge a SWAT team with a battering ram.

She desperately yanked the knob. When nothing happened, she clawed at the door, running her hands up and down it as if searching for another lock to turn.

"Might as well give up," he called out. "You're not getting those doors open."

Perhaps out of desperation, she pounded on one of the glass panes that was far too small for her to be able to get through even if she could have broken it, which she couldn't. She swore and yanked on the knob again.

"Steel bars," he explained.

She finally stilled, then slowly turned to face him. "What?"

"The doors. They're solid steel. Metal bars slide into them from the top and bottom when I press one of these buttons." He held up the same multifunction remote he'd used earlier. "Security is a pet peeve of mine. When you've seen the things I have in my career, you tend to be extra cautious."

Her lips pursed and she crossed her arms in a show of bravado. "Holding someone against their will is kidnapping."

"True. But it's completely legal, given the circumstances. I'm making a citizen's arrest of an armed intruder for breaking and entering." He pulled his cell phone out of his pants pocket. "Should I call the Gatlinburg police or Ranger McKenzie?"

Her face went pale. She started toward him, then stopped, as if debating her next move. "I'd appreciate it if you don't call *anyone*. I'm no threat. And I'm *not* armed." Her face reddened. "Not anymore." She held her empty hands out from her sides. "I'm not a burglar either. I didn't come here to steal anything."

"Really? Then explain the necklace you're wearing."

Her right hand moved to her chest, outlining the compass through her shirt. "It belongs to me. I was taking it back."

"It's evidence."

"Evidence of what? It's got nothing to do with that guy trying to kill me this morning. It's a piece of jewelry I lost in the woods."

"The park rangers and Gatlinburg PD might disagree. They're looking for you."

She frowned. "Why? Because I brought a gun to a national park? If I hadn't, I'd be dead right now."

"Like the man who was shooting at you? The one in the morgue?"

She blinked, her expression one of shock. "The rangers *killed* him?"

He stared at her a long moment, trying to gauge her reactions. Her surprise seemed genuine. But she could also be an excellent liar. "He was already dead when they found him. Someone slit his throat. I don't suppose you know anything about that?"

"You think *I* killed him?"

"Did you?"

Her answering glare reassured him. Her anger seemed genuine. And the way she'd stiffened told him she felt insulted he'd even asked. It was hard to envision her slitting someone's throat. But he still needed to hear her answer, to judge for himself whether she truly had nothing to do with what Ranger McKenzie had described over the phone earlier this evening.

"Skylar, I'm sorry to even ask, but I have to know that—"

"I didn't kill him, okay? The last time I saw him was when I was with you. I swear." Red dots of color darkened her cheeks. "Not that anyone should condemn me for it if I had. It would have been self-defense. He's the one who went after me." She drew a shaky breath, clearly rattled. "Who was he? Do you know?"

"A local hoodlum with a history of petty theft, vandalism, assault. Attempted murder's a step up in his budding criminal career, but not entirely unexpected given the direction he was headed."

"Budding? How old was he?"

"Why does his age matter?"

"Just curious."

Since he couldn't think of an advantage in not sharing that information, he told her. "Nineteen. High school dropout. He's been in and out of juvie since his first arrest three years ago."

A look of pain flashed across her face. "He would have been fourteen then. Too young. It's not him."

He considered her reply, and the possible implications. Had something happened nearly *five years ago* that had to do with her being targeted this morning? "Too young to be *him*? Who's him?"

Regret wrinkled her brow. Clearly, she'd said more than she'd intended. "Long story."

"I like a good story."

"I didn't say it was a good one."

He couldn't help smiling. "The necklace stays here.

Like I said, it's evidence." And it was his only leverage to try to gain her cooperation. The mystery of who she was and why someone had tried to kill her this morning was something he was determined to solve. Especially since he'd nearly gotten killed too. He wanted to know what was going on. And he wasn't about to stand by and do nothing, knowing a young woman had a target on her back.

Her hand went to her chest again where the compass dangled tantalizingly between her breasts. She really was a beautiful woman, even without makeup or fancy clothes.

"Please, Adam—"

"Trent. I told you to call me Trent."

"Yes, well, that was before you locked me in here, back when you said we could be friends."

"We still can be. Return the stolen property and I'll forgive the breaking and entering."

She backed toward the door, shaking her head. "You don't understand. The necklace means everything to me. I can prove it's mine. It has my name on it."

He set the remote control on the end table. Her wary gaze followed his every move.

"The name engraved on the compass is Sky." He settled onto the couch, trying to make her more comfortable, less afraid.

"Short for Skylar." Her gaze flicked to the remote. Even though she was too far away to try to grab it and unlock the doors, she seemed to be debating doing just that.

"Skylar what?"

She frowned. "Sorry?"

"Your last name, your real one this time."

Her jaw tightened. "Doesn't matter. Only my first name is on the compass. But I swear it's mine. It was a high-school graduation gift from my father." She advanced toward the couch, but stopped a good ten feet away. Still too far to make a dive for the remote. "Please. Let me go. And let me keep what's mine."

"The necklace? Or the gun?"

Her brows arched. "Both would be nice. But I'd settle for the necklace."

He shook his head.

Her cheeks reddened again. "I'd taken off the necklace by the stream to bathe. The gunman surprised me and I had to run, leaving my necklace behind. Later, when I went back for it, you'd taken it."

"How did you know it was me?"

"I saw you. I was hiding in the bushes."

"Then you, what, searched the Internet to figure out my home address, planning to break in and take it back?"

"Something like that."

He couldn't help but admire her honesty. "Where did you get Internet access? It's spotty up in the mountains, especially in the park."

"I...borrowed the access."

"Hijacked someone's Wi-Fi to use your phone?"

She shrugged.

He watched her, the truth dawning. "You don't have a phone, do you? Or a computer?"

She didn't answer. She didn't have to. It made sense she'd have neither. She was living off the grid, keeping her location and identity a secret. Having a phone, any electronics with GPS capabilities, could put her in danger of someone tracking her down. Which meant she'd used some other means to go online.

"My cabin isn't the first one you broke into today, is it? Any other criminal activities I should be aware of?"

"I didn't hurt anyone. Why should you care anyway? You're not a cop."

"Yes, well, some would say once a cop, always a cop. Kind of like the Marines, I suppose."

They watched each other like adversaries in a chess match. Waiting. Planning their next moves. Her nonchalance about all the laws she'd broken, just today, intrigued him. She didn't strike him as someone who'd been raised in desperate conditions, where stealing might seem like the only option just to survive. Something had happened to push her across that line, to make her comfortable breaking into houses, *borrowing* other people's property, and whatever else she did in order to leave no electronic trail. What had made her that desperate? And why was a well-spoken, obviously well-educated, intelligent woman living in the woods like a homeless person?

"After your Internet search, once you knew where I lived, why didn't you knock on my door and ask for your necklace instead of breaking in?"

"Would you have given it to me?"

"No."

She crossed her arms. "What do you want from me?"

"Your last name."

She swore. "I already told you, when we were in the woods."

"And...since you're not repeating it, I'm guessing you forgot that lie."

Her gaze faltered.

"You *did* forget the bogus last name, didn't you?"

"That's ridiculous."

"Is it?"

She stared at him a long moment, then arched a brow. "Anderson."

He burst out laughing. "Bonus points. You remembered. Good save."

"Trent—"

"I already searched every database I could think of for a Skylar Anderson. That's not your last name. Have a seat. Make yourself comfortable. All of the exits are locked electronically, steel bars, steel doors. Not just the French doors off the deck."

She glanced toward the front door behind him, and the bank of windows on either side. "I suppose the windows are secured just as thoroughly as the doors?"

"Of course. All the panes are acrylic, the same kind used to hold back millions of gallons of water at Ripley's Aquarium in Gatlinburg."

"Unbreakable. At least, through ordinary means. Doesn't that make you nervous? What if there's a fire and your fancy remote control has dead batteries? Or it's in another room and you're trapped with only a window as your escape?"

"It's what they call a smart house. Fire safety protocols are built in. I'd be able to get out."

"How? Some kind of secret override? A hidden panic button in every room?"

"It wouldn't be a secret if I told you, would it?" He

smiled. “And if you think your questions have diverted me from noticing that you’re slowly advancing toward my remote, think again.”

She fisted her hands at her sides. “If you were going to call the police, or the rangers, you’d have already done it. What’s your game?”

“No game. I just want to talk, to help.”

“By keeping me prisoner? That’s your idea of helping?”

Her defiance was apparent in the stiff way she held herself. Maybe, in order to convince her to trust him, he needed to trust her first. Hoping he wasn’t making a mistake he’d later regret, he picked up the remote control and pressed a button.

“The doors are unlocked. You’re free to leave.”

She whirled and ran. He cursed his foolish instincts as she threw open one of the French doors.

“Skylar, wait! *Please*.”

She paused on the threshold, looking back over her shoulder. “You said I could go.”

He slowly moved toward her, stopping as soon as she took a step onto the deck. Edging the front hem of his shirt up, he revealed the holster on his belt, and the pistol inside it.

Her eyes took on an accusatory look. “Going to shoot me now?”

“You’ll notice my gun is still holstered. I’m just showing you that I *could* have shot you, if I’d wanted to. In my line of work, I’m always packing.”

“You weren’t this morning.”

He laughed. “True enough. I tend to follow the law about not bringing guns into national parks. It’s a character flaw. As I said, I could have shot you if I'd wanted, the moment you broke into my home. I truly mean you no harm."

She glanced longingly at the deck stairs leading to the ground below.

"How long have you been on the run?" he asked. "Weeks? Months?" Her lack of response had his stomach dropping. "*Years?* Has it been years, Skylar?" Alarm bells began to go off in his mind and puzzle pieces clicked into place. "You mentioned the gunman would have been too young five years ago. Please tell me you haven't been on the run for *five years*." When she still didn't respond, he shook his head, incredulous. "Has it really been that long?"

"My life and what I've been doing are none of your business."

"What you've been doing became my business when we got in that gunfight together. Come back inside. Tell me what's going on. Maybe together we can find a way for you to stop running, once and for all."

She snorted in contempt. "If it was that easy, don't you think I'd have figured it out for myself by now? When all this started, I went to the cops. Several times. They couldn't help me. What makes you think that you can?"

"Fair question. I could tell you it's because I was a far better cop than most, that I'm stubborn and refuse to give up until I solve whatever mystery I'm working on. But you don't know me well enough not to assume I'm just cocky and bragging, so I'll add this. My confidence isn't solely based on experience. It's based on the latitude I have because I work for a private company. I'm not constrained by police procedures or governmental red tape. Unfinished Business is well-funded. We've got resources law enforcement only dreams about. Give me a chance. Let me help you live a normal life, to not look over your shoulder everywhere you go. Don't you want to interact with people, talk to them, have them listen to you, without worrying they might recognize you and put you in danger because of whoever's after you?"

She blinked. "How did you know?"

"That you feel isolated? That you long for normal human contact?"

She slowly nodded.

"How could you not? You've been living in fear for a long time. Maybe we can end that. All you have to do is trust me."

A single tear slid down her face and she quickly wiped it away. "I don't even know you. How can you expect me to trust you? This could be a trick. Maybe you're in league with whoever's after me."

"If I was, do you really think I'd have helped you today, risked my life? I'm not one of the bad guys, Skylar. I truly want to help."

The anguish in her expression had him wishing he could hug her and offer her comfort. He wanted to confess that he was a sucker for underdogs, that he couldn't stand for a woman to be in danger, that his curiosity was on fire to solve the mystery of who wanted her dead and why. But offering a hug, or more platitudes, wasn't going to convince her. He needed to *do* something, *show* her, prove to her that she didn't need to fear him.

He held up his hands, then carefully pulled her pistol out from his waistband and turned the grip toward her.

Very slowly, he moved forward and set the gun on the kitchen island ten feet from the open door. Backing up again, he stopped in front of the couch.

"If I was one of the bad guys, if I wanted to hurt you, I wouldn't return your weapon."

Her gaze flitted toward the island, then back at him, to the gun holstered at his waist. She seemed to be weighing the odds of reaching her gun before he could draw his own.

Sighing, he slowly pulled out his pistol and then tossed it onto the far end of the couch, out of his reach.

No sooner had it bounced onto the cushions than she ran to the kitchen island and grabbed her gun—pointing it at him.

He raised his hands in the universal sign of surrender, disappointment a bitter taste in his mouth. "Not very nice of you. But my offer still stands. If I can't convince my boss to let me help you on the clock, I'll do it on my own time. But knowing him, I can't imagine he wouldn't want to help someone in your circumstances. It's your choice. Go back into hiding now that you have your necklace and your gun, and you can keep running and hiding indefinitely. Or..."

She stepped backward toward the open doors, the muzzle of her gun still trained on him. "Or?"

"Or you can trust the man who didn't shoot you when he could have. The same man who just gave you your freedom, and your weapon, and threw his own gun out of reach. I'm trusting you, Skylar. With my life. I'm asking you to do the same. If you stay, we can try to figure this out, how to reclaim your life. But if you go, you'll still be in danger, constantly wondering—"

She whirled around and ran out the door.

Chapter Six

Trust him?

Skylar sat on a log deep in the woods, shaking her head in disgust at the gun in her hand. Her worthless gun. Trent had given it back, but it didn't matter. He'd taken out the magazine without her knowing, apparently when he'd grabbed her pistol from her backpack. Now, even though she had more ammunition, she couldn't load it since she didn't have another magazine. Saying he was trusting her with his life was a lie.

Then again, hadn't he done exactly that at the park this morning? He'd drawn the gunman's fire, risking his own life for hers, a complete stranger, all because he saw someone in need.

She shook her head. It didn't matter. He'd proven she couldn't really trust him when he'd risked nothing by giving her back an unloaded gun.

But she'd pointed that gun at him, proving *she* couldn't be trusted, hadn't she?

She groaned and rested her head in her hands, her elbows propped on her knees. Everything was so messed up. At least he'd been true to his word about allowing her to leave. He hadn't come after her. Which had her wondering all over again about his real intentions. He'd insisted he wanted to help her. If that wasn't true, wouldn't he have kept her locked inside, called the police, turned her in? Instead, based on her telling him that the police hadn't helped her in the past, he'd set her free. Didn't that prove he really was, as he'd put it, one of the good guys?

She could really use a good guy right now. Someone else to lighten the burdens she'd been carrying on her shoulders for so very long.

A mosquito buzzed around her head before landing on her arm. She slapped it, leaving a bloody trail. Grimacing, she wiped her hand on some leaves. Another night in the woods, without proper shelter or running water didn't appeal to her at the moment. And she couldn't risk going to a motel, not with Trent and his buddy rangers possibly looking for her. She was stuck right here. As if to punctuate that thought, her stomach rumbled, again.

In answer, all her backpack yielded was another energy bar. As an occasional snack, they were fine. But as many times as she'd had to consume them as her entire meal, she was beginning to hate them. Particularly with the memory of that mouth-watering steak she'd smelled at Trent's home. Steak. She couldn't remember the last time she'd had something that delicious. Did he have any leftovers he wouldn't mind sharing? Now that could be a good reason to go back.

Or to get the magazine for her gun. Maybe both.

She hefted her pistol again, shaking her head at her own stupidity. It was far lighter than usual, something she should have noticed when he'd given it back to her. But she'd been too intent on escaping to notice.

In spite of her aggravation, a rare smile twisted her lips. The way he'd taken her gun so effortlessly and ejected and hidden the magazine without her seeing him do it was enviable. No doubt her father would have been impressed. With Trent. He'd have been disappointed in her.

Today had been a screw-up from beginning to end. She was lucky to be alive. Lucky to have the compass. And she had Trent to thank for both of those blessings. If one of the rangers had picked up her necklace, she'd probably have never gotten it back. But Trent had let her take it, and keep it, even though he'd been armed and didn't have to.

Another mosquito buzzed around her head. She swatted at it, then grabbed her backpack and stood, facing the direction that would take her to Trent's cabin. If she went that way, she was turning over her destiny to someone else, someone she barely knew. She turned around, facing the thick, dark woods. If she continued that path, it would be more of the same. Loneliness. Danger. With no end in sight. But at least her safety was in her own hands.

She turned around again. Forward? Or backward? Which way should she go? She turned again, her shoulders slumping in defeat. Giving up had never sounded so good.

Plopping down on the fallen log, she rested her head in her hands again, mulling everything over.

What should I do, Dad? What should I do?

A long time later, a peace she hadn't felt in ages

settled over her, inside her. She let out a shuddering breath and raised her head. Pressing a hand to her chest, she felt the comforting circle of the compass through her shirt. There might be enough moonlight filtering through the trees overhead so she could read the inscription. But she didn't have to see it. The inscription was burned into her mind, her heart, her soul.

One more, Sky. Just one more. You can quit tomorrow.

All her life, she'd taken those words literally. She'd believed they meant she had to rely on herself, and no one else. But her father had loved her, deeply. He'd wanted her to be safe, to survive, to live. She wasn't living. She was merely existing, minute by minute, hour by hour, in a constant state of fear. She'd done exactly what her father didn't want her to do. She'd quit, on life. It was time to take charge again. To find joy. To end this miserable existence and be happy. And there was only one way she could think of to make that happen, by turning to the one person who'd ever truly expressed interest in helping her.

Adam Trent.

Hefting her backpack more securely into place, she stood and started through the woods.

She glanced up at the sky, but clouds obscured the stars. She didn't know what time it was. Late, obviously. Midnight? One? He'd probably gone to bed. Or was he searching for her?

A few moments later, she stepped from the tree line onto his driveway. The house was dark. Was he asleep? Would he be angry if she woke him? She straightened her shoulders. If he was, then she'd take it as a sign that coming back here was a mistake. Being alone, running, always looking over her shoulders really sucked. But she'd survived this long on her own. There was no reason to think she couldn't keep doing what she'd been doing. Even though she really, *really* didn't want to.

She headed up his driveway toward the house. This time, she used the front door. Still wary about this whole idea, she pressed the doorbell. If he didn't open the door in about a minute, she'd go.

Shifting on her feet, she glanced at the windows to the left and right of the door. Still dark. Had it been a minute yet? She let out a deep breath. Probably. Definitely. And the longer she stood under the bright porch light, the higher the risk that someone might drive by and see her. She'd already risked a lot by going to a motel earlier to use one of their business center computers, especially knowing that whoever had sent the gunman might be in town trying to find her again. Not to mention the rangers. She really needed to get out of the light.

She was about to turn away when the front door swung open. Then, she was too stunned to do more than stare, and try not to drool.

Trent stood in the doorway wearing nothing but a pair of jeans sagging low on his glorious, lean hips, the top snap undone as if he'd hastily dressed and had forgotten to fasten it. Above the tantalizingly low waist of his jeans were golden, rippling abs and a broad chest lightly matted with dark hair. His biceps bulged as he braced both arms against the door frame on either side of him, blinking his compelling, deep blue eyes as if he was still trying to wake up.

"Skylar?"

She cleared her throat, trying to get her brain firing again. Hormones she didn't remember having were standing at attention and painting all kinds of erogenous pictures in her mind—of her, and Trent, together.

Good grief, get a grip, Sky.

She forced herself to meet his gaze instead of ogling him like a starving person at a buffet, wanting to dive onto the table—or onto Trent.

"I, um…you have my gun magazine." Not what she'd meant to say, but at least she didn't do something really embarrassing, like trail her fingers down that dark line of hair on his abdomen, down, down, all the way to his—

"That's why you came back? For a gun magazine?" He shook his head, clearly disappointed and headed into the main room. A moment later, he returned and handed the magazine to her. "There you go. You've got what you came for. Enjoy running for the rest of your life, however long that might be."

"You're being cruel."

"I'm being honest." He stepped back as if to close the door.

"Wait."

He stopped, his hand on the knob. "What? What else?"

She clutched the magazine. "Thank you for returning this. But that's not really why I came back." She drew a shaky breath. "I want to hire you."

His brows arched in surprise. "Hire me? To do what?"

"Solve a murder."

He frowned. "Whose?"

"Mine."

Chapter Seven

After putting on a shirt and grabbing his laptop out of his home office, Trent settled onto the couch beside Skylar. He opened a word-processing document to take notes and paused with his fingers over the keyboard. "Ready to explain what you meant about hiring me to solve your murder?"

She drew a shaky breath. "Before I answer your questions, I have one for you."

"Okay."

"First, to set things straight, I didn't break into someone's cabin and borrow their computer or their Wi-Fi like you thought earlier. I went to a motel today and used a computer in their business center. I paid for the computer time too. In spite of what you may think, I'm not in the habit of stealing. And when I shelter somewhere, like that cabin in the National Park, it's because it's basically abandoned. No one lived there. I wasn't hurting anyone by being there."

"I wasn't judging you. I was trying to figure out the facts. But I shouldn't have made assumptions. My apologies."

She looked surprised. "Thank you. I appreciate that."

"What did you want to ask me?"

That look of wariness entered her eyes again as she twisted her fingers together in her lap. "You already know that I looked you up on your company's website. After that, I searched the county's property appraiser website to get your address."

He chuckled. "I'd wondered how you got my address. Good sleuthing. I should have put my deed under an LLC to prevent others from figuring out where I live so easily."

"I'm glad you didn't or I'd never have found you." She waved her hand in the air as if waving away her words. "Unlike most people, you're definitely careful about not putting personal details on the Internet. I couldn't find any social media accounts under your name." Her troubled gaze met his. "You mentioned being a cop in Chattanooga. That was also on your bio on your company's website. So I searched for references to you specifically in Chattanooga. I wasn't trying to be nosy, not exactly. I needed…reassurance."

"That I wasn't one of the bad guys?"

"Something like that. Anyway, the local newspaper there did stories on you or I probably wouldn't have found anything. You were quite the detective. All kinds of medals, accommodations, awards from citizens groups. Solved a lot of high profile cases. What I couldn't figure out was why you quit and moved to Gatlinburg. Why throw away that career success to start over as a private citizen here?"

He frowned. "As you said, I don't tend to put my personal life in cyberspace."

"I'm not trying to pry. I mean, I am, but I'm putting

my life in your hands by even being here. I need to know that I'm not making a mistake. If you were fired—"

"You're worried I was a dirty cop?"

"I didn't say that."

But she was thinking it, wondering about it. And he couldn't blame her. He had locked her inside his home and threatened to hand her over even though it was obvious she was worried about her safety if he did. Someone had tried to kill her, just this morning, and they weren't the first. It was understandable that she was wary, even though she'd risked everything to come back to his house. Understanding her motivation and feeling bad for her were the only reasons he decided to answer her question.

He sighed heavily. "I wasn't a crooked cop. I certainly wasn't fired. I quit. And it had nothing to do with the job. It's personal." At her look of disappointment, he sighed again and told her the short version, the only version he was willing to share. If it wasn't enough, then so be it. Some things were too personal, too intimate, to tell a relative stranger.

"A few years ago," he said, "in Chattanooga, my life as I knew it ended. My wife was killed. I needed a fresh start, somewhere else, where I didn't see her face every time I drove down a familiar street or went into a restaurant we used to frequent. That's why I left. That's the only reason I left."

She pressed a hand to her chest. "I'm so sorry. I didn't mean to bring up painful memories."

Since he thought about Tanya every single day, she wasn't exactly resurrecting memories. But he still had to tamp down a flash of irritation that she'd pried. He didn't talk about his wife with anyone, except Callum and a few others he was close to at work. But someone he'd just met, never. Until now.

He poised his hands over the keyboard again. "Can we get back to why you're here? Explain what you meant about solving your own murder."

She watched him a long moment, perhaps put off by his abrupt change of subject. But he refused to tell her more about his private life. And he certainly didn't want to get into all of that at one in the morning.

Finally, she nodded, as if accepting what he'd told her and deciding to move on. "It's a long story. I don't really know where to begin."

"Let's start with your name. We both know it's not Skylar Anderson. I searched every database I could think of for that combination and found nothing, not here, and not in Chattanooga either."

She blinked. "Why would you search Chattanooga data for me?"

He smiled. "You obviously think you're a better bluffer than you are. When I told you in the Smoky Mountains park that I used to be a cop in Chattanooga, your eyes got big and round. Either you were worried that I was a former cop, or that I came from that area. Either way, it got my Spidey senses going and I dug in. But, as I said, I got nothing. Who are you? Your real name this time."

She cleared her throat and motioned over her shoulder toward the kitchen. "I don't suppose you have any leftover steak I could have. It smelled so good earlier."

"You're avoiding and delaying."

"I'm hungry."

He laughed, then sobered. "There's a steak in the fridge you can heat up, *after* you answer my question."

Her chin tilted at a defiant angle. Stormy brown eyes met his gaze as she finally told him what he'd been wanting to know all day.

"It's Skylar, Sky for short, like the engraving on the compass. But my last name is..." She swallowed. "My last name's Montgomery."

As she hurried to the kitchen area, he slowly closed the laptop. He didn't need it. Her name had set off a kaleidoscope of images flashing through his mind. The memories he'd tried so hard to remember since the shooting this morning finally came into focus. *Skylar Montgomery.* It wasn't possible. Was it? He watched her as she took a plate out of the refrigerator and put it in the microwave.

She looked to be the right age, about thirty, maybe a little younger. Petite, the right height to match those pictures in his mind's eye. The hair was different though—shorter, reddish-brown. The woman from the news reports and police reports had long, wavy dark hair, nearly black. But that was the first thing people changed when on the run, their hair style and color.

"From Chattanooga?" He called out, watching her body language to judge for himself if she told the truth this time. "You were an only child, lived in California. San Diego. After your father died, you moved to Chattanooga, right?"

She half-turned, looking at him as the steak heated. "You already got all that on your laptop?"

He shrugged, not bothering to tell her it was from his memories of the case he hadn't worked but that everyone in his department knew about. It had been all over the news too. He should have put the pieces together long before now. But like most people, he'd thought Skylar Montgomery had died after being chased by a gunman into the Cherokee National Forest. Her body had never been found, but the bullet holes in her car and blood evidence on the trail were compelling. She'd eventually been declared dead. That was almost five years ago, which matched up with her earlier concerns about the gunman's age in the park today.

He waited to question her until she rejoined him on the couch, setting a bottled water beside her on the end table and the plate in her lap. The first question he wanted to ask died unspoken as he watched her obvious pleasure as she took her first bite of steak. She closed her eyes, relishing the flavor as if she'd never had anything that good in her life.

Once she'd wolfed down nearly half of it, he asked a different question than he'd originally planned. "When's the last time you had steak?"

She chased her most recent bite with a drink of water before answering. "Honestly, I can't remember. I usually live off energy bars and other nonperishable foods I can eat on the run."

"You said you went to a motel earlier today. Don't you ever eat in restaurants?"

"Too crowded, too dangerous. Someone might recognize me."

"Your case did go national. I suppose someone around here might remember, if they saw what you look like now and were still able to make the connection. But since you supposedly were killed—which is the murder you're saying you want me to solve, right?—then I don't see how they'd make that leap in logic. You can't be leaving an electronic trail to follow or the police wouldn't have declared you dead. I'm sure they would have tagged your accounts to see if there was any activity after you disappeared."

"I've seen enough TV shows, and heard enough lectures from my father, to know not to use any credit or debit cards. I pay for everything in cash."

"For almost five years? Where'd you get enough cash to last that long? And how'd you pull it out of the bank initially without the police seeing the activity?"

She smiled. "I've got my dad to thank for that. He was a bit…overprotective and didn't trust banks. He amassed a small fortune over the years, was quite successful. But he never opened a bank account. He had a safe at home and that's where he kept his money. Out of tradition, and respect for his constant warnings about always being ready for an emergency, I kept a safe too and put the money he'd saved in there. That's how I've stayed off the grid all this time, by using that cash. I hide the bulk of it as soon as I get to a new place, and put a small amount in my backpack for my supply trips. If I were to ever run through my dad's money, I have an account no one knows about, set up under an alias. But I've never had to access those backup funds. Aside from the fear of electronic trails, even with it being set up under an alias, it never felt right."

"Why not? It's your money, isn't it?"

"Technically, yes. But the way I got it feels smarmy." She shot him a warning look. "No, I didn't steal it."

"Wasn't going to say you did."

Her look turned grateful and she nodded in gratitude. “A hospice patient gave it to me. I was a nurse, in my former life. Got tired of the long hours at a hospital and went to work in the claims department of an insurance company. They hire a lot of former nurses to examine claims looking for fraud. It wasn’t exciting, but the pay was too good to pass up. Still, I missed the hands-on part of helping others. So I compensated by working at hospice on weekends.”

“You became a hospice nurse in addition to your regular job?”

“No. I volunteered there. Not in a medical capacity, but as a companion. I’d visit with patients who put their names on a list, wanting someone to talk to. Often they either didn’t have any family, or the family they had rarely came to see them. That’s how I met Martha, a sweet older lady who was the epitome of the perfect grandmother. Just a wonderful woman. Long story, but after she passed away, her lawyer set up an account for me with a hefty amount of cash. I tried to refuse, but he said it meant a lot to her knowing I’d be taken care of, that she loved me like a granddaughter.”

She pressed a hand over her heart. “Not having family of my own anymore, that felt too good to ignore. So I quit arguing. I always figured I’d follow up with her family at some point to return the money. I’d never met any of them. But obviously if they came to see her much, she wouldn’t have put her name on the companion list, hoping a stranger would come talk to her. So sad. She was such a sweet, interesting woman. Her loved ones missed out not being there.”

She waved a hand in the air. “I’m droning on, don’t

mean to. My point is that, yes, I pay everything in cash and have plenty of it. I'm not hurting. And I have Martha's fund as a fallback plan. So, no, I'm not foolish enough to leave an electronic trail for my would-be killer to use to track me. I honestly have no idea how he keeps finding me."

"You obviously didn't get lost and freeze to death like the police concluded years ago when you ended up in the Cherokee National Forest."

"Oh, I definitely got lost. Normally, in a situation like that, I'd have guided myself using the stars at night and would have made my way back to civilization. But I'd lost a lot of blood, wasn't thinking clearly. I think I was feverish. Took weeks to make my way out of the forest."

"Normally? You can map by the stars?"

"My dad was Special Forces, an Army Ranger. Drilled his training into me since I was a little girl, as if I was one of his men."

He vaguely remembered something about her father being in the military. It was a blessing he'd taught her survival skills or she probably wouldn't be here right now. "You mentioned blood loss. The police theorized that the man who shot your car shot you too. But they weren't sure."

She nodded. "Right through my side. Thank God it missed everything vital. But it bled like crazy, got infected."

"You obviously found your way out of the forest. Why didn't you go to the police? Why did you let everyone believe you were dead?"

"I didn't have any family to worry about me. And it was the third attempt on my life. I knew whoever was behind the attacks would try again, and again, until he succeeded. But if he thought I was dead, maybe I'd have a chance. I made my way back to my house, broke in through a rear window so no one would see me, took my backpack of essentials, and ran. I've been running ever since."

"It was the third attempt on your life? I only heard about the one."

"Yeah, well. The other two didn't involve massive search-and-rescue efforts, so I guess they never made the news."

"Good point. The media ate up the story about the police finding your bullet-riddled car in the parking lot and a blood trail."

She shivered and set her plate on the side table, no longer interested in the rest of her food. "It was crazy. I was driving home when some guy tried to run me off the road. Then he started shooting. When I ended up in that parking lot, I realized my mistake. It was a dead-end. But his car was coming up the road fast. All I could do was get out and run."

"Earlier you said the guy who shot at you today was too young, that he'd have been about fourteen five years ago. Were you wondering if he was the man who'd pursued you into the Cherokee forest all those years ago?"

"I wondered, of course. But I can't imagine a kid that young making his way to Chattanooga to try to kill me. He's not the guy who went after me back then."

"Did you get a good look at him? The guy from years ago?"

"I was too busy trying to get away, to survive."

"But it wasn't the first attempt on your life."

"No. Someone tried to kill me a couple of other times in Chattanooga. And since then, too, like today. Somehow, whoever wants me dead always seems to find me. I can go months, went a whole year once, before another attempt on my life. I think it may have been the same person initially. But over the years, he's been hiring others."

"Like the kid this morning."

She nodded. "I assume so, yes."

"Someone must have a powerful motivation to want you dead, to keep pursuing you so long. Is there an abusive boyfriend in your past? Ex-husband? Someone who feels you wronged them and they want revenge?"

She shook her head. "The only serious boyfriends I've had were in high school. Just a few flirtations and occasional dates in college. I was too busy working on my degree and starting my career to get serious with anyone. And no, I've never done anything to anyone that sticks out in my mind. I honestly have no clue why someone has made my life a living hell. All I can do is keep moving from place to place, trying to keep my head down."

"What about your life in California? Could it be someone there who followed you to Tennessee?"

She shook her head. "I don't think so. I wanted a fresh start, kind of like you did moving here. Both my parents had passed away. I had no reason to stay. I suspected my mom may have been from Chattanooga, in spite of how secretive my parents were about their past. So my first choice was the University of Tennessee. When they accepted me, that's where I went, not that I ever discovered any long lost relatives. But it was years later that the first attempt was made on my life, a gunman across the street from the hospice center where I volunteered. As soon as I saw him, I knew something was wrong. You mentioned your Spidey senses. My dad was like that, could sense when something was wrong, when he was in danger. He did his best to train that into me and I guess it worked. That guy was…off…the way his attention was zeroed in on me. I dove to the side maybe half a second before the first shot went off."

He shook his head in wonder at her close call. "I don't remember hearing or reading about that, and I was with Chattanooga PD at the time."

Her nose scrunched in a disgusted expression. "Not surprising. The detective looking into it didn't take it all that seriously. The hospice center was outside of town, in a rural area. Apparently there've been other complaints about gunshots heard in the woods before and it always tracked back to some hunter getting too close to the center, not meaning any real harm."

"Where were you when this happened? Near the building?"

"Close enough that a hunter shouldn't have been firing in that direction. I was at the edge of the parking lot, heading to my car. And, yes, the detective had me half-convinced it was accidental too, that maybe the man was looking at a deer or something and didn't notice me. But since someone tried to shoot me again a few weeks later, I didn't have a lot of faith that the first incident was an accident. By the time I was chased into the Cherokee National Forest, I knew someone was determined to kill me and wasn't going to stop until I was dead. After being shot, I ended up feverish, delirious and lost, fighting to survive, for three weeks. When I finally made my way out, I had decided to go to the police, but the little café I stumbled into had the news on the TV above the counter. Everyone was watching, didn't notice me, as the reporter talked about the search being called off and that the police believed I was dead. I turned around and left. I realized it was a gift, that if the police thought I was dead, then the man trying to kill me might too."

Hearing the awful things she'd endured had him aching to pull her into his arms and reassure her. But she'd run from him once. He doubted she'd welcome his touch, no matter how well-intended. Carefully maintaining his professional, calm demeanor, he asked, "How long after that café incident did someone go after you again?"

"Not long. Maybe a month. But I figured it was because I'd been foolish. When I'd returned to my house for money and supplies, he must have been watching the place and followed me. Since then, I've been far more careful about not going anywhere familiar to me. I constantly move around."

She covered her mouth to stifle a yawn. He figured that was his signal to quit badgering her with questions, for now. They both could use some sleep. He set his laptop off to the side and stood, offering his hand to pull her up from the couch.

"Let's get you set up in the guest room. You're about to fall asleep mid-sentence. We'll talk more in the morning."

Her gaze searched his. "Then…you'll help me? You'll let me hire you to solve my case, get my life back?"

"I need to talk to my boss, move some things around on my schedule. But yes, I'll help you."

She surprised him by throwing her arms around his waist and hugging him. But before he could even put his arms around her and return the hug, she was pushing away, her cheeks flushed pink.

"Sorry," she said, not meeting his gaze. "Don't know what made me do that. I'm just…grateful."

"Everyone needs a hug now and then. If you ever want to finish that hug, I'm here."

She blinked, looking wary again.

He sighed, wishing he knew how to make her more comfortable around him. He deeply regretted locking her in earlier. At the time, he'd half-suspected her of killing the gunman and had every intention of turning her over to the rangers. But it hadn't taken long to realize that she was solidly in the victim category, definitely not a murderer. And that she needed help. Serious help.

He stepped back to give her room. "Come on. I'll show you where everything is."

She gave him a tentative smile, grabbed her backpack and followed him down the hall.

Chapter Eight

Once Skylar was settled in, Trent headed to his office on the opposite side of the house, next to the garage. After shutting the door, he sat as his desk and made a call.

Five rings later, the call was answered, with some choice swear words. “Someone had better be dying,” Callum gritted out. “Do you have any idea what time it is?”

Trent grinned at the sound of his friend’s grumpy voice. “Didn’t wake you, did I?”

“You’re kidding, right? It’s two, no, two *eighteen* in the morning, on a workday. This had better be good.”

“When does Hamilton County come up in the rotation to have one of their cold cases worked?”

“Hamilton County. Where the heck is…wait, Chattanooga?”

“That’s the one.”

“Heck, I don’t know. No time soon. We just finished prioritizing the next batch of cases and Hamilton County wasn’t in the queue yet. Why? What’s going on?”

“I want to play my pet-project card and work a cold case for Hamilton County. And I want to choose which of their cold cases to take.”

“That’s not how the pet-project card works. You have

to look at the list of cases coming up in their queue and choose one of the cases they *want* us to work, not some random investigation they may not even care about or may already be working on their own. Why are you calling me about this anyway? Ryland's in charge of this stuff."

"Ryland's on vacation, starting today. You're his backup this week."

"Oh for the love of… His plane doesn't fly out until late morning. You can call *him*. He's probably home right now, in bed, like me."

"But you're already awake."

Callum swore. "You're afraid he'll tell you no."

"*Afraid* isn't the word I'd use. But, you know how the saying goes. Sometimes, it's easier to ask for forgiveness—"

"Than to get permission. I know, I know. One of your many mottos to live by. You're going to get both of us in trouble. You know that, right?"

"It's important, Callum."

"It had better be. What case couldn't wait until morning and is worth getting your best friend in hot water?"

"Skylur Montgomery."

"Who?"

"Skylar Montgomery. A couple months shy of five years ago. Her car was shot at and she managed to park it and run into the Cherokee National Forest. The gunman chased her. One of his shots went through her side, but she managed to get away. When the rangers came in response to shots-fired calls, the gunman must have given up pursuit. They followed the blood trail, got search and rescue involved, called the whole thing off a few weeks later."

"Wait. Skylar. Isn't that—"

"The woman in the shootout this morning, in the Great Smoky Mountains National Park."

"The one who almost got you killed."

"No, the idiot shooting at her almost got both of us killed."

"Hold it, hold it. We talked about this earlier. They found the gunman dead. Your ranger friend, McKenzie, wants to interview her about it. He thinks she killed him."

"She didn't do it."

"You have proof of that?"

"I'm a good judge of character. She insisted she had nothing to do with his death, and I believe her."

"She insisted? She disappeared this morning before they even found the dead guy. Dang, Trent. She's there with you, isn't she? What exactly are you getting me into here?"

"You're in the clear. I'm neither confirming nor denying that I know where she is. You can't get in trouble since you don't know anything."

"No one's going to believe that. This is a career killer. Not to mention a potential aiding and abetting charge."

"She's not a fugitive. No one has issued an arrest warrant."

Callum said a few choice words. "They have a BOLO out on her as a person of interest. Every law enforcement officer in the county has been told to be on the lookout for her. Don't split hairs. You're in dangerous territory. Are you sure this is the hill you want to possibly die on?"

"No question."

"That was quick. No hesitation."

"She's innocent, Callum."

"Really? Just how pretty is she?"

It was Trent's turn to swear. "That's got nothing to do with my decision."

"You sure about that?"

"Give me some credit. I'm not a pathetic horny teenager trying to get laid. She's been on the run for *five years*. There have been multiple attempts on her life, and she's got no one in her corner. She's an only child. Her father's dead. No living relatives. And the police in Hamilton County never took her seriously. She's desperate. I'm not going to throw her to the wolves. She needs our help."

"The police can help her. All she has to do is go downtown and tell them what happened."

"If it was that simple, the police would solve every case they ever get and none of them would go cold. This is the cold case we should be working on, because we can actually prevent a homicide instead of finding the killer after the fact. We can save a life. If we turn her in, they'll lock her up for defending herself and might even railroad her into a murder charge. How long do you think she'd last in county lockup before her killer finds her and bribes one of the inmates to shiv her? A day? Two?"

"Look, Trent, I get that this is important to you. That's coming through crystal clear. What I don't get is why. All of our cases are important, and we do save lives. Every time we take a killer off the streets, we keep him from claiming another victim. You need to let the police do their jobs. If you don't turn her in, if you hide her and work on her case, what happens when this all comes out? Even if you don't end up in jail, you could severely damage our company's reputation with the law enforcement agencies whose support is critical to our mission. Our boss may even fire you. Grayson can't allow one rogue investigator to destroy the company he built. You need to let this go. Do the right thing and turn her in."

"I never told you about Tanya, did I, Callum?"

Silence, then, a moment later, "Your wife? That Tanya?"

"That Tanya. I never told you how she died."

"Ah, man. You don't have to do this."

Trent sighed and scrubbed the stubble on his jaw. "I need you to understand. I won't go into the details except to say that she was murdered by a man who'd been bothering her at work. He was stalking her. She told me this guy was being a jerk and she got bad vibes around him. I told her to report him to her supervisor because I was too busy doing my job to really listen. If I had, I'd have realized he was more than a jerk. He was a sociopath. And if I'd just done a simple background check on him, I'd have found all the red flags I found *after* he killed her."

"Trent, I had no idea. I'm so sorry. I—"

"No sorrier than me. But that doesn't bring my wife back. I didn't do what I should have done to help her when I could. And now here's another woman being stalked, with proven instances of someone actually trying to kill her. I couldn't live with myself if I turned her over to someone else to protect her and she ended up dead. I have a hard enough time facing myself in the mirror every morning as it is. I can't tell her no, Callum. Whether you help me or not, I'm in this, with the support of Unfinished Business, or without."

"You'll have our support. I'm behind you a hundred percent. All of us are, or will be, once I explain everything. I'll talk to Grayson in the morning, see what he can do. Gatlinburg PD owes him, big time for all the help we've given them on their cases. They may jump at the chance to look the other way and call it even. And that McKenzie guy is a good friend of yours. I'll talk to him too, see what he can do to de-escalate the situation. Regardless, don't worry about it. We'll figure this out. We'll notify Hamilton County, let them know we're re-opening the investigation immediately. I don't guess there's any reason to send Willow there as our victim's advocate like we usually do before working a cold case. You said there's no family to notify."

"Right. A victim's advocate won't be necessary this time. And when you speak to the Hamilton County liaison, be careful. Make sure they know this needs to be kept on the down-low. The fewer people who know I'm digging in, the better, at least until I get a feel for who might be involved."

"Hold it. Are you saying you think Chattanooga PD is involved in some kind of cover-up regarding Skylar Montgomery?"

"Not at all. I worked with them for years and never had any reason to suspect corruption. But this was a huge media circus years ago. I don't want to risk loose lips letting something slip and stirring up a firestorm that could interfere with my ability to get the information I need. Whoever's behind this could go into hiding and I might never catch them."

"What's the plan, then? You're bringing her to the office in the morning to review the case with the team?"

"I haven't confirmed or denied to you that I know where she is."

"Screw the double-talk. I'm already in this and only getting deeper. Are you bringing her in?"

"There's no point. I already checked our files. We don't have one for this case. The liaison will need to quietly get the case file from the police and send it to you. But I don't want to wait for that. Once you have it, notify me and I'll pull up the information online. You and the team can review it on your end without me and we'll discuss it later. Skylar and I are leaving this morning."

"Leaving? Where are you going?"

"Back to where it all began. Chattanooga."

Chapter Nine

Skylar stared across the back deck table at Trent and slowly lowered her forkful of scrambled eggs. “That’s your plan, take me to Chattanooga so the guy who wants me dead will more easily find me?”

“Guy or girl. You don’t know who’s behind the attempts on your life. We need to keep an open mind.”

She rolled her eyes and tossed her fork onto her plate, her appetite gone. “An open mind is one thing. Leading me to certain death is quite another. I might as well paint a target on my back and stand on top of Lookout Mountain with a neon sign that says Shoot Me. This was a mistake. I’m leaving.”

Pushing back from the table, she grabbed her backpack from inside the French doors. She’d repacked after her shower earlier, per her habit, always ready to run. She just hadn’t expected she’d be running again quite this soon. After adjusting the straps, she turned to head down the deck stairs, then froze.

Trent was standing near those same stairs, watching her with a guarded expression. And beside him was a man she recognized from yesterday, when she’d peered at him through some branches—Ranger Adam McKenzie.

Both of them watched her intently. Trent, with that same guarded expression. McKenzie with a face as hard as granite, his right arm resting on the holster at his waist.

"Don't run." Trent's voice was calm, soothing. "McKenzie isn't here to arrest you."

She glanced at the opening to the stairs, but there was no way she was getting past these two tall, brawny men. Hopping over the deck railing wasn't an option either. She'd fall all the way down the mountain. The French doors were still open. She took a quick look. That remote control of Trent's was inside on the end table. The remote that could lock the doors behind her, then unlock the front door when she reached it. She'd have a head start. Maybe it would be enough for her to escape into the woods.

She looked back at Trent.

He glanced at the opening, then at her, his deep blue eyes narrowing in warning. "Don't."

She ran inside and slammed the doors shut, managing to flip the lock on the doorknob just as Trent grasped it. Behind him was Ranger McKenzie with an amused look on his face.

"Skylar, this isn't what you think," Trent yelled. "Open the door." He rattled the doorknob again, then slammed his shoulder against it. The entire frame shook. Another hit or two and it would crash open.

Unless she got those steel locks in place to reinforce everything.

She ran and grabbed the remote.

Trent rammed the door again. The wood made a popping sound.

She frantically ran her hands over the buttons, searching for the right one. There! She pressed the one labeled Doors.

A metallic clicking noise sounded just as Trent hit the door again. This time, it didn't budge. She looked at him through the panes and saw his face was red as he straightened, rubbing his shoulder. He looked angry enough to hit her, and she wasn't about to hang around to find out whether he was the hitting type. McKenzie was no longer standing behind him. Had he headed down the deck stairs to cut her off?

She turned and ran for the front door, hitting the unlock button as she grabbed the doorknob. She threw it open and tossed the remote on the ground before sprinting toward the woods on the opposite side of the house from the deck.

The sound of shoes pounding on the ground behind her confirmed her fears. McKenzie, or Trent, or both were after her. And dang, were they fast. But she'd scoped out the area all around Trent's cabin before approaching it that first time. She knew what logs were down, where the wet marshy areas were, when to zig and when to zag to avoid thorny bushes.

Always have an escape route mapped out.

Her dad had taught her that. And she'd been following that critical rule for years.

The pounding footsteps were closer, closer. But the woods loomed just up ahead. She was going to make it.

A lone shadow suddenly appeared separate from the

tree line twenty feet in front of her. It was a man, and he was holding a gun by his side, but at the ready.

She skidded to a halt, slipping and sliding on the pine needles, nearly falling. When she straightened, the man smiled and tipped his head in greeting.

"Name's Callum. I presume you're the infamous Skylar Montgomery."

The pounding shoes stopped on either side of her. Trent grabbed her right arm. McKenzie grabbed her left and pulled out a set of handcuffs.

"You won't need those." Trent's voice was hard. "Isn't that right, Skylar? You're going to cooperate and come inside to talk. And you're not going to run. Agreed?"

She swallowed and glanced back and forth between the three men, vaguely wondering if all of Trent's male friends were tall and muscular like him. Callum and McKenzie certainly were. Since the odds of her escaping all three of them were pretty much zero, and her choice seemed to be to go with them willingly or in handcuffs, she nodded at Trent.

"I won't run." *For now.*

He pulled her away from the ranger, and the three of them headed up the lawn toward the house.

Chapter Ten

Trent shut the office door behind him and Skylar, leaving Callum and McKenzie waiting in the main room.

Skylar whirled around to face him, her cheeks fiery red. "Is that your idea of showing someone they can trust you? You ambush them?"

He stepped around her and plopped down in the leather chair behind his desk. "I was going to give you an update after breakfast. But you took off. Again."

"Taking off, as you call it, is the only thing that's kept me alive. If I perceive a threat, I'm gone. Period. Your buddies out there are most definitely threats. I'm leaving here the second this conversation is over. Unless you plan on stopping me, again, and letting that ranger handcuff me and haul me off to jail for having the gall to have survived someone trying to kill me."

"No one's cuffing you, unless you try to run."

Her eyes practically shot sparks at him as she dropped her backpack onto the floor and crouched in front of it.

He swore and jumped up, swiping her backpack before she could get anything out of it. "Let me guess. Going for your gun? That won't make all of this go away. It'll only make it worse."

She clenched her fists in frustration as he took out her gun and ejected the magazine. After putting the magazine in his pocket, he shoved the gun into her backpack and tossed it on one of the two wing chairs beside her.

"Sit down," he ordered.

She stiffened, her brown eyes narrowing.

"Please," he added, making a concerted effort to tamp down the aggravation in his voice.

Instead of sitting, she crossed her arms. "I suppose if I run out of your office, those other two jerks will chase me down."

It was hard not to let his own anger flare in response to hers, especially given all the trouble he and his friends were going to for her. But he reminded himself that she'd been through hell. She had every right to be upset and feel betrayed because she didn't know the facts. Taking a deep, calming breath, he sat behind his desk again.

"Those two *jerks*, as you call them, are both risking their careers to *help* you."

A frown wrinkled her brow. She was about to say something, but he held up a hand to stop her.

"Let me explain." He motioned toward the empty chair. "Please, Skylar."

She said a few choice words, but relented and sat.

Progress.

"Callum, one of my *buddies* out there, is a coworker. I woke him very early this morning to update him on my plans to work your cold case. I could take a leave of absence, do it on my own, but if we have my company's backing we'll have more resources. Callum has been going to bat with our boss on your behalf and got him to agree not only to let me officially work your case, with his support, but also to pull some strings with the local police to get them to cancel the BOLO on you."

"I don't…what's a BOLO?"

"A communication blast, basically. It goes out to law enforcement in the area, letting them know to be on the lookout for someone—in this case, you. It means that every cop in the county has your description and will arrest you on sight. Or they would have, if Grayson Prescott, my boss, hadn't convinced the police chief that we're handling this and not to arrest you."

She blinked, looking less angry. "O…kay. Didn't expect that. I—"

"The main reason Grayson was able to get the chief's cooperation was an agreement that you would meet with Ranger McKenzie. The deal is that you'll answer his questions, provide fingerprint and DNA samples to cross-check against the murder scene, so he can perform due diligence and assure *his* boss that you're not actually a killer."

"Hold it. I didn't agree to that. And I didn't kill—"

He held up his hands again. "I'm on your side. You've got nothing to prove to me. But McKenzie needs some convincing. You don't have to talk to him. That's your choice. But if you don't, the deal is off."

"And he arrests me."

"Unfortunately, yes."

"Some deal."

Trent crossed his forearms on top of his desk and gave her a hard look. "It's a sweet deal. And it wasn't easy to arrange. All you have to do is answer some questions."

"And provide my fingerprints and give a DNA sample."

"Is there a reason that should worry you?"

"Did you forget the part where I'm believed by most people to be dead? What if he runs my fingerprints or DNA profile through some database and it alerts the wrong person that I'm still very much alive?"

"The fact that someone tried to kill you recently means whoever's after you already knows you're alive. But I get that you want to stay below the radar, keep your location secret. Are your fingerprints and profile on file somewhere to even compare to?"

She hesitated, then, "That's a good question. I don't know. Wait, yes, I was fingerprinted as part of my background check years ago to become a nurse."

"Unless you were charged with a felony, that shouldn't be an issue. Background checks aren't used for loading people's prints into AFIS." At her confused look, he clarified, "The FBI's Automated Fingerprint Identification System. It's a national database for maintaining fingerprint information to help law enforcement. You've got nothing to worry about."

"So you say."

"Like I said, it's your choice. Give McKenzie what he needs and this will all go away. He's smart, reasonable, an excellent investigator. There's no incentive for him to put the wrong person away for a crime, or to compromise your safety. He's more than ready to be done with this so he can eliminate you as a person of interest in his case. Then you and I will be free to work on *your* case."

"I'm not going to Chattanooga."

He sighed. "We can discuss that later. For now, you need to talk to McKenzie. This is all highly irregular and doesn't exactly follow standard policies and procedures for either agency we're dealing with, not to mention my own company. So when we walk out of here, it might be a good idea to start by thanking McKenzie and Callum both for giving you this chance." Tired and aggravated, in spite of his best efforts, he didn't wait for her reply. He stood and crossed to the door, but looked back before opening it. "Ready?"

She slowly stood and wiped her hands on her shorts, straightened her top, then shrugged her backpack on. Either she was bracing herself to take off when he opened the door, or she was nervous about sitting down with McKenzie. Or something else had her anxious. His belief that he could read people and predict what they might do in a given situation had been on shaky ground ever since he'd met this complicated woman.

A much calmer, almost hesitant Skylar crossed to stand in front of him, her hands looped through the straps of her backpack. "Why didn't you tell me all of this before your friends—"

"Callum and McKenzie."

She nodded. "Why didn't you tell me before they showed up? You had to know I'd get spooked, take off, or Callum wouldn't have been outside waiting just in case I ran."

"You weren't the only one who was surprised. I got a text about the deal just a few minutes before we sat down to eat. I figured I'd call and set up a meeting with

McKenzie once I spoke to you. I haven't had a chance to ask the two of them why things changed, but I think it's a safe bet we can lay that at Callum's feet. He didn't want to risk that I'd take off with you before he and McKenzie had a chance for an interview."

"I don't understand. Why would he think you'd do that?"

"Because he knows I believe in your innocence, and I think it's a load of crock that you should have to submit to an interrogation because the guy who tried to kill you wound up dead himself. I'd have argued for another compromise. But that's not an option now. Let's get this over with, and then let's catch a bad guy together and give you back your future. What do you say?"

She placed her hand on his arm. "Thank you. For believing in me."

Her grateful smile, along with her warm, soft touch had his heartbeat kicking up a notch. Maybe Callum was right about her looks influencing him. It had been far too long since he'd made time for a relationship, even a casual one. And Skylar was exactly his type—whip-smart, incredibly competent, and curvy in all the right places.

He cleared his throat. "No need to thank me. You risked your life to save mine this morning. That alone convinced me that you're a good person."

She winced. "*Good person* might be open to interpretation." She set her backpack on the chair and unzipped a side flap. When he saw what she was pulling out, he swore.

"I know, I know. Sorry." She turned the second gun around and handed it to him, grip first. "I wasn't stealing. I was borrowing. Last night, I searched your place after you went to bed and found this in a drawer. I didn't want to be unarmed if you took my magazine again—which you did."

He shook his head in exasperation as he slid the gun into his pocket. "I can see why you lasted on the run for so long. You're unpredictable."

"Not unpredictable enough, or gunmen wouldn't have found me several times over the years. Do you really think going to Chattanooga is the right thing to do?"

"It's dangerous. I'm not going to lie and say it isn't. But staying here's dangerous too. The person trying to kill you knows you're in Gatlinburg and is likely searching here for you right now. Getting you out of town makes sense. And visiting the original scene of the crime, where your cold case started, is one of the best ways I know to get traction on any case. I can't promise it will be completely safe. But I'll do everything I can to protect you, no unnecessary risks."

She cocked her head. "I appreciate that. One more question. Why? You told me you left Chattanooga to get away from the memories. Why would you put yourself through that pain again for me?"

He smiled. "If you ask Callum, he'll tell you it's because I'm a sucker for a beautiful woman."

"Don't patronize me."

"I'm not. You *are* a beautiful woman."

"Stop it. Don't insult my intelligence by trying to distract me from my question. I want to know the real reason you're willing to go back to a place that reminds you of your wife. You said you moved to get away from the painful reminders of her. It doesn't make sense that you'd be willing to return for a woman you barely know."

A knock sounded behind him. "Trent?" Callum's muffled voice carried through the door. "Everything okay in there?"

"We'll be right out, Callum."

"Ranger Rick is starting to think you let his person of interest climb out a window."

Skylar rolled her eyes and stepped to the door. "We're making mad passionate love on top of the desk. Tell Ranger Rick to give us a couple more minutes for our happy ending."

A choking cough sounded on the other side of the door, followed by quick footsteps leading away.

Trent grinned. "The top of the desk might be a bit uncomfortable to make mad passionate love. The rug in front of the window's pretty well-padded though."

"I'm still waiting for you to answer my question."

He blew out a deep breath, his amusement evaporating. "It's *because* of my wife that I'm willing to go to Chattanooga with you."

Her brow furrowed in confusion. "I don't—"

"I let her down. Tanya, my wife. She needed me, and I wasn't there for her. That's a burden on my soul every single day. You came to me in need, and I'm going to do everything in my power to protect you, to give you back your life. That's why I'm willing to return to the town I freaking hate. Because I truly think it's the only way we're going to get the answers we need to make you safe, once and for all."

She searched his gaze, as if judging the truthfulness of his reply. Then, she nodded and grabbed her backpack. “Once the interrogation is over, we’ll do it your way. We’ll go to Chattanooga. But I don’t like it and, honestly, it scares me to even think about being there. I’ll stay one week. After that, if you haven’t figured out who’s trying to kill me, I’m gone.”

Chapter Eleven

Skylar sat at the dining table across from Trent in the eating area adjacent to the kitchen, alarmed and somewhat bewildered at the activity going on around her. She'd assumed that once she'd answered McKenzie's questions, he and Callum would leave and she and Trent would head to Chattanooga. Instead, after ushering McKenzie out, Callum led two other men inside—more coworkers from Unfinished Business.

One of them, Asher Whitfield, smiled at her in greeting and then carried a small black bag through the doorway behind her. Skylar looked over her shoulder and realized it was the garage. She just managed to glimpse him pulling out a screwdriver as he rounded a dark-colored SUV before the door closed.

Brice Galloway, the second man, reminded Trent he needed a picture as soon as possible. Then he wheeled the rolling suitcase he'd brought with him around the corner into the foyer, presumably heading to Trent's office.

"Picture?" Skylar asked Trent at his seat across from her. "Is he referring to me?"

"Yes. We'll need a current—"

"Trent?" Callum called out from the family room. He shoved his phone into his pocket. "Ivy will be here soon. Can you help me for a sec?"

Trent smiled apologetically at Skylar. "Sorry. I'll explain what's going on in just a minute. Be right back."

"But I don't—"

"Trent?" Callum said again.

"Really sorry. Things are coming together faster than I expected. Hang tight." Trent strode into the family room to speak to Callum. Whatever they were discussing had Trent typing something on his phone. Was he texting someone? Or looking up something on the Internet? His "just a minute" turned into five and still he didn't return. Trent put his phone down and both men started messing with the cords and knobs attached to the electronics on the shelves beside the massive TV over the fireplace.

Skylar was tempted to pick up her backpack from under the table and sneak out the front door. She was nervous enough that her face had already been seen by four people aside from Trent this morning. And now apparently another one, Ivy, was on the way here. This certainly didn't go along with her desire to keep her existence a secret. But Trent had told her before that he'd use the company's resources—which included their people, she supposed—to help with her case. But that didn't make her feel any less worried. The only reason she wasn't running right this second was because of something that was helping to counteract the anxiety, something she hadn't felt in a very long time.

Hope.

And her pledge to give Trent a week. He'd complained

it was too short. She'd told him it was far longer than she felt comfortable with. So they'd shook on the agreement. She was putting her life, and hope for a real future, in his hands. But she wasn't going to blindly follow his lead. If he wouldn't take the time to discuss what he and his coworkers were doing, she'd see if she could figure it out on her own.

Unfortunately, she didn't have a cell phone to look up anything on the Internet. It hadn't bothered her before. But right now she wished she could use one to at least review the Unfinished Business website again and read more about Callum, Asher and Brice. Oh, and this Ivy woman who was coming over.

The door behind her opened. Asher stepped inside, but he didn't give her a chance to ask him any questions. Another quick nod was all she got as he hurried past the table toward the foyer carrying the same black bag he'd had earlier.

"Plate's ready," he called out to Trent.

Trent waved his acknowledgment and Asher disappeared around the corner, followed by the click of the front door opening and closing.

Skylar was about to call out to Trent herself and demand the explanation he'd promised. But he was on the phone now. Callum was turning various knobs while Trent turned on the TV. A laundry detergent commercial was replaced by the view of a conference room. But there weren't any people present, just a long table with chairs around it. Was that Trent's company? Was he going to have a video meeting with someone there?

The doorbell rang.

Before Skylar could win the debate with herself on

whether it was safe to answer, Trent jogged to the foyer, sliding his phone into his pocket as he disappeared from view. Again, Skylar heard the front door open and shut. Then a man and woman walked into the main room with Trent, stopping just short of the couch.

The man was tall, thin, dressed all in black, and had a modern short hairstyle that would have seemed conservative except that it was lime green. Alarm bells started going off in Skylar's head. This wasn't the kind of guy she'd imagine worked for Unfinished Business. She remembered the website bragging about their investigators all having law enforcement backgrounds. She couldn't picture this guy fitting that bill, not just because of the hair either. He seemed…nervous, out of place. And he was staring at her as if trying to memorize her every feature. If she had ammunition in her pistol, she'd probably have gone for it then and there. She really needed to get her magazine back from Trent.

The woman with lime-green guy was blond, pretty and nearly as tall as Trent. Both of the newcomers, like almost everyone else who'd come to the house so far, carried large black bags with them. Trent gestured to the doorway to the right of the fireplace and the three of them headed through the opening and down the hall that led to the bedrooms.

Skylar cursed beneath her breath. Callum was still fiddling with the TV controls. Now there was a man on the screen, sitting in the conference room. There wasn't any sound, which she guessed was the issue that Callum was trying to fix, since both he and the man appeared to be talking to each other on the phone.

Skylar was through waiting for Trent to answer her

questions. She'd figure out the answers on her own. Quietly getting up from her chair, she was careful not to draw attention. Intent on figuring out what Asher had been doing, she slipped into the garage. The big clue was him telling Trent the plate was ready. Sure enough, when she checked she saw that the license plate on the back of the SUV didn't say Sevier County as it would for someone living in Gatlinburg. Instead, it said Hamilton, the county she'd fled when she left Chattanooga.

After carefully pulling the garage door closed, she passed through the dining area around the corner into the foyer. The office door was shut, but she didn't bother knocking. She shoved open the door and headed inside.

Brice was typing on a laptop at the desk. He arched a dark brow in question, his fingers curled over the keyboard.

"Don't let me interrupt whatever you're doing there." She smiled, glanced at the documents the printer on top of the desk was spitting out, then plopped into one of the wing chairs. She noted the other equipment on top of the desk, equipment that must have been in the rolling suitcase he'd brought.

"Ms. Montgomery, is there something I can help you with?"

"Actually, yes. Can you confirm for me that you're—"

"There you are." Trent shoved the door open. He nodded at Brice, then held out a hand to Skylar. "Got a minute?"

She ignored his hand and crossed her arms. "Not really. Brice and I were about to have a conversation. I'd rather stay here and see if he'll answer my questions since you don't seem inclined to bring me up to date about my own cold case."

Brice's eyes widened and he looked suspiciously like he was trying not to laugh.

Trent narrowed his eyes at him before looking at Skylar again. "My apologies. I'll fill you in on our way."

"On our way?" She stood. "Are we leaving now?"

"Not exactly."

"Trent—"

"I'll answer all of your questions. Promise. Just come with me."

She sighed as he grabbed her hand and tugged her out of the office. He continued to pull her along with him through the family room. There were more people on the TV screen now, milling around the conference room. Before she could ask about that, he ushered her into the hallway. The people she'd seen earlier must be back here. And with everything she'd seen in the past few minutes, she was starting to understand what was going on. Or, at least, she thought she did. It was time to find out if she was right.

"I've already packed what little I own in my backpack if you're taking me to the guest room to get my stuff," she told Trent. "Well, except for my gun magazine, which I expect you'll return soon."

He grinned. "As soon as we're out of shooting range of my friends, I'll give it back." He motioned for her to enter the guest room where she'd slept the night before.

When she saw what was waiting for her, and who, her suspicions were confirmed. But she decided to make Trent suffer a little for making her figure everything out on her own. She whirled around as if to leave. Unsurprisingly, Trent stepped in front of the open door, blocking her exit.

"Hang on a sec, Skylar."

She crossed her arms. "You've been telling me to hang on for the last half hour, promising to explain what's going on. Now you drag me into a bedroom where another couple is waiting. Whatever kinky thing you've got in mind, you can forget it."

His eyes widened.

Feminine laughter sounded behind Skylar.

"Knock it off, Ivy," Trent warned, aiming an aggravated glance over the top of Skylar's head. He cleared his throat. "That's not what this is, I swear, Skylar. I should have warned you. We aren't, that is, I mean they're not… I'd never—"

She winked.

He gave her a suspicious look. "Why do I feel that I'm being made fun of here?"

"Because you are." She turned around. "You're Ivy Shaw, right? I recognize you from the company website."

The blonde smiled and shook her hand. "I sure am. Nice to meet you, Ms. Montgomery. This is Max. Don't let the green hair fool you. He's very discrete and a master hairdresser." She motioned to the man behind her who had a bewildered expression on his face. Since he was clutching several pairs of scissors in one hand and combs in the other, Skylar didn't try to shake his hand.

"Max, good to meet you." She turned to Ivy. "When do we get started on my makeover so no one will recognize me?"

Ivy chuckled. "Right now, I guess. Max approved

the large sink in the attached bathroom. Said he'll have plenty of room to work. He was just sorting through what supplies to take in there. We'll use that rolling desk chair and—"

"Excuse us a minute." Trent grabbed Skylar's hand and tugged her into the hallway.

This time it was her turn to hold up a hand to stop whatever he was going to say. "No need to explain anything now. I've figured it all out."

"Oh? What do you think you've figured out?"

"Well, you did say that your boss had agreed to let you work my cold case in your official capacity, with help from your company. Since so many of your coworkers have been here this morning, they're obviously here to do exactly that, help with the case."

She counted using her fingers as she stated each point. "Asher switched the license plate on your SUV with a Hamilton County one, so we're driving that to Chattanooga without the red flag of a Sevier County plate to draw any attention."

He leaned against the wall, crossing his arms.

She checked off another finger. "Poor Callum has been trying to figure out your audiovisual equipment to get a conference call together with your people at the office. I think he's just about got it working, by the way."

"I'm so relieved," he answered drolly.

Another finger was checked off. "Brice is printing fake documents and wants that up-to-date picture of me to finish my fake driver's license or ID card, I'm guessing. I noticed he was printing a lease under assumed names. We're apparently going to be Mr. and

Mrs. Trent Adams. I see what you did there, switching your first and last names."

He shrugged. "Makes sense since everyone calls me Trent anyway. It'll help us both not to slip up too easily when someone asks my name."

"I'm still Skylar then?"

"Unless you want something different. It's not a very common name, but not so exotic it will stand out too much."

"Thanks. I think. Moving on. Ivy, I'm guessing, brought along the case files you wanted from Hamilton County. And she also brought Max, of course, to change my appearance before we take that picture that Brice needs."

Trent looked at her with what she could only describe as grudging admiration.

"How'd I do?" she asked.

"When this is over, I'll give you a job application to be an investigator for Unfinished Business."

"Score. Did I leave anything out?"

"Only that Ivy is also going to stay with you and Max while he does your hair. Not that he's a threat, but he's not one of ours, so there's only so much I'll trust him. She'll watch over you. I'd also like to know how you figured out those documents Brice is printing are for new identities. I went into the office two seconds after you did. That wasn't enough time for you to read through everything he was working on."

She shrugged. "This isn't my first jog around the block. I recognized the typical fake ID paperwork and the laminating machine beside the printer."

"And why would you recognize all that?"

"Montgomery isn't my birth name. It's an alias."

He glanced past her at the open doorway where Ivy and Max were talking in low tones, then motioned for her to move up the hallway with him a few more feet.

"Are you saying when you were living in Chattanooga, it was under a fake name?"

"Well, it's the name I was going by for several years. I didn't think of it as fake. It wasn't like I was trying to fool anyone about my education or experience. It's just the last name I had when my father died."

"But it wasn't your birth name."

"No. It was an alias my father created for me, for both of us. He had all the equipment, like Brice has in your office. And contacts who could help him create the things he couldn't."

"You're talking social security cards, birth certificates?"

She nodded. "With those two things you can pretty much get anything else you need, including a real driver's license. But he had to improvise a few times, thus the laminating machine and special paper and printer like Brice has, to create a temporary driver's license with the hologram things on them like the real ones."

"What was your birth name?"

"No idea. Wallace is what's on my birth certificate. But Dad told me years later the names on that were just as fake as the names that came later. I remember a McAlister in there somewhere, one *L*, not two. And it seems like there was a Smith at one point. And don't look at me that way. My father wasn't a criminal. I told you he was an Army Ranger, a good man. But something happened when we were stationed over-

"We moved several more times before settling in San Diego. I was Skylar Montgomery through all of high school. Mom had passed away by then, and I think Dad was more consumed with grief than whatever paranoia he had about someone finding him. And before you ask, no, I never knew what he was afraid of exactly, or who. And yes, I've often wondered if it could have anything to do with why someone went after me later. But Dad had been gone for years before that happened. It doesn't make sense that someone would hang on to a grudge against my father that long and go after his daughter. Does it?"

"It's weak," he agreed. "But it's a heck of a coincidence, something we should explore. How many years are we talking since the last name change?"

"Trent?" Callum stood at the end of the hallway. "Brice needs that photograph to finish up. And everything's ready for the video conference. Want me to notify headquarters to go to the conference room?"

"I wanted Skylar at the meeting so she can answer questions." He glanced toward the guest room. "I don't have a clue how long it takes to cut and dye hair."

"Anywhere from an hour to two," Skylar told him. "I can tell Max to be as quick as possible and not try for perfection." She flipped her hair over her shoulders. "Am I going for blond, bright red, what?"

He eyed her hair. "It's a shame to change it. I think the reddish-brown looks great on you. But so did the nearly black you had before you went missing."

She blinked. "Um, thanks."

He cleared his throat. "Short and blond would be

completely different from long, auburn like you used to wear it. Does that sound okay?" he asked.

"If it means staying safe, I'd shave it all off."

He smiled. "I don't think we have to do anything that drastic."

"Short and blond, coming right up."

TRENT PULLED THE door shut to the guest room, then strode down the hall to Callum. "We'll postpone the full team meeting until tomorrow morning. Hopefully, by then we'll all have more information to share anyway." He motioned for Callum to follow as he headed toward his office.

When they stepped inside, Brice was on his phone behind the desk. "Lance, Trent and Callum are here. I'll call you back in a few minutes."

"Don't hang up." Trent closed the door. "I want to talk to him too."

"I'm putting you on Speaker." Brice set his phone on top of the desk.

"Hey, Lance," Trent said. "You still have contacts in Army Intelligence?"

"Officially, no. Unofficially, what do you need?"

"That's what I was hoping you'd say. Give me everything you can on an Army Ranger named Ryan Montgomery who was last stationed in Germany. Except, that's not his real name. You're going to have to do some digging. He changed his last name many times over the years after leaving the military. Before Montgomery it was Smith, McAlister, Wallace, and potentially other names."

"I'm good, but you've got to give me a little more

than that to go on. Can I assume Ryan Montgomery is related in some way to Skylar Montgomery?"

"He's her father, or he was. He died several years ago. His wife's first name was Abby. Skylar was their only child. When they left Germany, they moved to Lyon, France. Then they moved to Houston, Texas, some other places, and eventually settled in San Diego, California. I haven't seen the Hamilton County file yet. I'm hoping it has some background information on Skylar—dates and locations—that you can use to go backward. Or maybe you can go from Germany forward and build a dossier on the father from there. Based on a date range I'll send you from talking to Skylar, pull lists of Army Rangers stationed in Germany and see if you can whittle it down."

"It'll take more than one shovel to do all that digging, especially given the short time frame. A week, right?"

"Way less if we're wrapping this whole thing up at the end of a week." Trent shot a questioning glance at Callum.

Callum nodded in understanding and left the office.

"I'll try to buy us extra time," Trent said. "But we'll have to show some real progress to have any chance at getting Skylar to stick with us longer than that. She's nervous and antsy, especially about going to Chattanooga. Callum will be your second shovel. He's on his way to headquarters right now."

Brice sat back in his chair. "What's the father got to do with this?"

"Maybe everything, maybe nothing. He was paranoid, for years, constantly changing names and moving his family around. Now his daughter has someone after her. I want to know whether her father's paranoia is based on a real threat, and whether that threat could have passed on to his daughter. And I need that information yesterday."

"On it." Lance hung up.

Brice motioned toward a manila envelope. "I've got your new driver's license ready, registration and a copy of the lease for the rental house in Chattanooga. A credit card under your alias will be overnighted. That's not something I have equipment to do here."

"Tomorrow will be great. I shouldn't need the card, but it's good to have, just in case."

"I can have Skylar's license ready about twenty minutes after you get me that picture I've been asking about."

"She's in the guest room right now getting a makeover, so if anyone from her former life sees her, hopefully they won't recognize her. As soon as she's out, I'll snap some pictures and text them to you."

"Sounds good. Need anything else from me? You gave Lance and Callum marching orders. I'm feeling left out pushing paperwork."

"It's not just paperwork, and you know it. No one else around here can do what you do. But, yes, since you asked. How's your schedule looking for the next few days? There is something you could help me with. It's not easy, though."

"Easy's boring. Lay it on me." Brice pulled his laptop toward him. "What do you need?"

"That kid who tried to kill Skylar yesterday, I want to know who hired him and I'd really like to know who killed him. Answer those two questions and we've probably got the guy trying to kill Skylar. It's a tall order. Gatlinburg PD and the investigative park rangers are trying to find out the same things. I need you to find out what they know and go from there."

"Got a name for me or do I need to get that from the police?"

"Darius Williams, nineteen-year-old local. Figure out his movements in the days before he went after Skylar. Maybe you can narrow down a window of time when whoever hired him first made contact. If he visited Chattanooga recently, that would be huge. If he did, I can work the other end, track his movements, see where he went and who he might have met up with."

Chapter Twelve

Trent glanced at Skylar in the passenger seat of his SUV. Her eyes were closed, more out of boredom he imagined than her being sleepy. It was still early afternoon.

"Welcome to Chattanooga," he told her.

She blinked and looked around at the trees and hills rolling past her window. "Good grief. I thought we'd never get here. I could have made that trip in half the time. By taking major highways instead of all the Podunk two-laners you insisted on traveling."

He chuckled. "You didn't enjoy the scenery? All those rolling hills, horses, the rock-strewn mountains we traveled through?"

"If we were going anywhere else but here, I would have. One thing's for sure, your plan to make sure no one was following us must have worked. I don't think I've seen another car in hours."

"Do you always exaggerate this much or is it the blond hair affecting your personality?" he teased as he turned down yet another two-laner, as she called them.

She rolled her eyes and fluffed the wavy blond-striped curls that reached just below her ears. She'd messed with her hair many times during their drive, often checking the visor mirror.

"Stop worrying. You look great." She really did. He was more of a brunette man himself, but her new look had nearly stolen his breath when she'd walked into the family room. Ivy must have brought her some clothes too because Skylar was wearing a royal blue sundress with white flowers all over it and strappy white sandals. A small white purse hung from her shoulder. He'd been too stunned to speak and had used the excuse of gathering up the Hamilton County case file from the dining table to avoid talking until he was sure that he could. She made concentrating exceedingly difficult. It hadn't helped that a grinning Callum had whispered to him to wipe the drool off his mouth.

Skylar gave him a doubtful look. "You're just being nice. I think the blond stripes make me look like a hooker."

If he'd been drinking right now, he'd probably have spewed his drink across the dash. Instead, he laughed. "They're subtler than stripes. Max called them highlights, or something. And trust me, no one is going to mistake you for a hooker. That blue dress, the cut and color of your hair, they make you look…sophisticated."

"Sophisticated." She checked the mirror again. "Now that's something no one's ever accused me of before."

"No? Why not? You're…" He was going to say beautiful again, but he really needed to pull back on using those kinds of words or she'd think he was hitting on her. Never mind that he really wanted to. The timing, and situation, made those thoughts completely inappropriate. He just wished he could quit thinking them.

"I'm what?"

He glanced at her, then slowed to make another turn. "Smart. Clever. A great marksman."

"You sound like my dad."

"Ouch. Never had a woman accuse me of that before. I must be losing my touch."

She laughed. "Trust me. I don't mean it the way you took it. 'Cause you definitely don't make me have daddy types of thoughts." Her face flushed a light pink, reassuring him that he might not be the only one fighting this attraction. Misery loved company, and he was happy to share.

She cleared her throat. "What I meant is that my dad would think those things you said—intelligence, marksmanship, being able to figure things out—are the best attributes to strive for. You saying that, honestly, it feels good. Reminds me of what's important. Being independent and taking care of myself." She frowned. "Normally, anyway. Turning my fate over to you this week is…difficult, embarrassing even."

He reached over the console and squeezed her hand. "Never be embarrassed to accept someone's help. It takes a strong person to recognize when they need help, and to take it. It's *because* you're intelligent and clever that you reached out. And together, we'll get through this. We'll find out why someone's after you and put a stop to it. For good."

When he would have pulled away, she surprised him by threading her fingers through his. "You really believe that, don't you? That you'll figure this out, make me safe?"

"Of course. We're a good team. And I've got a great team backing me up."

"I sure hope you're right." Still obviously a little embarrassed, she pulled her hand free. Seeming to suddenly notice their surroundings, her brow wrinkled in confusion. "Where are we? I've never been in this area before."

"You sure about that?" He slowed and took yet another turn. "We're almost there. Still don't recognize it?"

"Recognize what? I really don't think I've... Wait. Some of these houses look familiar. But nothing else. If I'm supposed to recognize this area then things are really jumbled up because it's not matching any of my memories."

"I imagine a lot's changed since you lived here. This used to be one of the east side's most rural roads, with only a handful of homes. Now there are quite a few houses nestled back on these big lots, as you can see. But the place you'll remember best is at the end of the road, with enough trees between it and any neighboring homes to still make it feel isolated."

"How would you know that? Have you been here before? Or some time recently?"

He shook his head. "I haven't been in this part of Tennessee since I left a few years after you. But I had a contact here scout it out this morning for me, send photos. You'll see for yourself as soon as we pass this last clump of trees."

"I don't think so. I mean, some of those houses struck me as familiar. But overall, this road really doesn't..." Her eyes widened as a small parking lot came into view with a sprawling one-story, red brick building behind it. A portico covered the entryway and displayed the words Hamilton County Community Hospice & Palliative Care across the front.

She clutched the armrest, tensing in her seat. “What are we doing here?”

He slowed and turned into the parking lot, heading toward the far left side. “Don’t panic. It’s safe.”

“Are you kidding me? The last time I was here a guy across the street took potshots at me.” Her face visibly paled as he pulled to the curb near some trees, a good forty feet from the building. “Why are you stopping right here, at this exact spot?”

“You know why. This is where you were when that man shot at you.”

She swallowed, then turned to face him. “I told you what happened, but you still couldn’t have known—”

“Exactly where you were standing at the time? Sure I could. Police reports. There was a drawing in the Chattanooga PD file, mapped out and measured.”

“That’s surprising. I didn’t even think they’d paid that close attention. The lead detective seemed married to the careless hunter idea. But the shooter wasn’t dressed like a hunter, no fatigues or orange reflective jacket. And no one’s stupid enough to fire across a parking lot full of cars, next to a hospice center.”

“Maybe he just didn’t care. If he was drunk enough and had chased that buck for a while and was frustrated, he might have fired anyway. When he missed the deer, he took off so he wouldn’t get in trouble.”

She frowned. “You really think a hunter accidentally shot three times so close to me that I had to dive for cover, but wasn’t trying to hit me?”

“Given the later attempts on your life, no. You were

targeted. But I can understand the detective trying to come up with alternate theories to explain the man's behavior. You didn't have any known enemies. Or, at least, you didn't list any in the interview you gave at the police station. He didn't try to rob you. Even now, knowing he was trying to kill you, I'm stumped over what his motive could be."

"Okay, well, maybe thinking of the detective as a moron isn't fair once you explain it that way. But it didn't seem like he even tried to solve the case. He never called me with updates. I had to call him. And he didn't have any findings to report, just said the case remained active. It was only after a man shot at my car and almost ran me off the road that the detective came to see me again." She waved a hand, her brow creased with frustration. "Just tell me why we're here. What do you hope to accomplish? If the guy after me has some kind of connection to this hospice center, then—"

"Then that will be a good break in our investigation."

"And puts me in harm's way."

After putting the SUV in Park, he turned in his seat to face her. "This is where some of that trust comes into play. For starters, we took the back roads here to make sure no one was following us, except for one of our guys hanging a mile back, watching our six."

Her eyes widened. "We weren't all alone, like it seemed?"

"We had someone watching over us the entire trip. And while we were taking our time along those back roads to ensure no bad guys followed us, we were giving other members of my team a chance to beat us here, scope things out, get into position."

"Into position?" She looked across the parking lot. "Where? Here?"

He nodded. "Two aisles back, five spots over, the white sedan." He motioned with his hand. The driver sitting in the car nodded.

Skylar drew a sharp breath. "Is that Ivy?"

"Sure is. Look down the road, at the turnout past the end of the parking lot. See the guy in the dark green truck, pulled off to the side of the road?"

"No, I… Wait. Yes, I see him now. The truck blends in with the woods behind it."

"That's the idea. The man driving it works for us too, although not as an employee of our company. We hired him and a couple of others who live here in Chattanooga to help us this week. They work for a personal security firm we've worked with in the past, so they've been vetted."

"That definitely makes me feel better. But it also reminds me we haven't agreed on the fee I'm going to pay you for helping me. I got so caught up in things this morning, it didn't even occur to me. But what I can afford may not come close to covering the costs of all these resources you're using, not to mention the bag of new clothes Ivy brought me when she came to your house. I may have to break in to that fund Martha set up so I can reimburse you."

"We can talk money later. Don't worry about it."

She gave him a suspicious look. "You *are* going to take my money, right? I said I wanted to hire you. I'm not a charity case."

"We have other things to focus on right now, like touring the hospice center."

"Go inside? No way."

"I've got two people in the building right now. Ivy was in there earlier talking to the administrator, and she's going in with us. There's another guy in the parking lot too, one of the locals from that security company I mentioned. Those security guys know the area and this place. They've used cover stories to gain access, look around, see who all is here and whether anyone seems like a potential threat. And Ivy set up a tour for you and me as a couple interested in looking over the place for your aunt who may need hospice soon. Ivy's posing as a close friend of ours who's gone through this type of thing with one of her own relatives so she wants to support us through this. But her true purpose is to keep the person giving the tour busy with questions, giving you and me more leeway to look things over, see if anything triggers some useful memories."

"That sounds fairly straightforward. Shouldn't make anyone suspicious, I suppose."

"They do these tours all the time. Normally, they're scheduled in advance, so there was a little hiccup there. But a small donation helped the administrator find some flexibility in her schedule."

"Donation? Trent, seriously, I can't afford this—"

"We're back to that? I said don't worry about the costs of this investigation."

"And I told you I'm not a charity case. I mean it. While I'm not hurting financially, I have to be frugal so my money will last if this doesn't work out. Hiring you for only a week was intentional, to keep costs down. But with you bringing in so many people, hiring an outside security company, it has to be costing an enormous amount of money. And it's not like I can just run out and get a job to make up the difference and not keep my identity secret."

He sighed. "All right, we'll talk money so I can set your mind at ease. Have you ever heard of Prescott Industries?"

"Of course. They're a huge conglomerate of companies all over Tennessee. What does that... Wait. Is the owner of Prescott Industries your boss, Grayson Prescott? The owner of Unfinished Business listed on the website?"

"One and the same. He's a billionaire, Skylar, with a capital B. He didn't set up Unfinished Business to make money. He and Willow, his wife—who's also our client liaison—established the company to find Grayson's first wife's murderer. And after we solved that case, he continued with the charter, determined to help other families obtain justice for the cold cases that law enforcement doesn't have the resources to work. We partner with law enforcement, but it's Grayson's dime, not theirs. We do it pro bono for the counties we contract with. And we don't accept fees and never charge a family."

"But...but I hired you. We had a deal."

"We never agreed that I'd take any money. We made a deal that I'd help you, and in exchange you would help me. Having the actual victim of a cold case walk you through the various crime scenes and answer your questions is golden. It's an advantage I've never had before. You're doing me a favor—helping me solve a case for Hamilton County. If I do solve this, it makes me look good. It's a win-win for both of us. I should be paying you."

She rolled her eyes and smiled, easing back against the seat and seeming more relaxed. "You're being ridiculous. But I'm not going to argue against my good fortune. If a billionaire is willing to cover the cost, I'm not going to fight him about it. But please do tell him thank-you for me. That's a wonderful thing he does for families, helping to bring them closure on behalf of their loved ones."

"I'll let him know you said so."

She nodded her thanks and glanced at the white sedan, then the dark green truck down the road. "I do have to admit that knowing others are watching our backs is comforting." She drew a shaky breath. "Okay. What do you want me to do?"

"You stay with me the whole time. It's unlikely that anyone will recognize you. You don't look at all like you did when you volunteered here. And there's been a ton of turnover in the staff since then, as confirmed by our security team. My team and I will do everything we can to keep you safe. But, I won't ever try to force you to do something you're not comfortable doing. I'd like you to walk me through what you used to do here, where you used to go, tell me who you used to visit. Being in the same place, experiencing the same sights, sounds and smells could jog memories of details you never realized might matter. It could give us some leads to follow. But you don't have to. We can leave right now."

"I'll do it. You just surprised me, is all. If you'd let me know ahead of time..."

"You would have said no."

She stared at him a moment, then sighed. "You're probably right. Still, I'd prefer not to be ambushed like this yet again. We're supposed to be working together, partners. Promise me you'll keep me in the loop going forward. No more surprises, okay?"

"I'm the first to admit I'm not used to explaining my every move. But I understand your reticence, and your concerns. No more surprises."

"Just like that? You aren't going to argue?"

"Just like that. You're the boss. The next step is yours."

She glanced at the woods outside her window and shivered. Just when he thought she was going to tell him she couldn't do it, she popped open the door. "Let's get this over with."

Chapter Thirteen

"What did you say your aunt's name was again, dear?" the administrator asked Skylar as they stopped in the main hallway by the opening to the cafeteria.

The panicked look on Skylar's face told Trent she'd forgotten the name of her fake aunt that he'd given her as they'd walked into the building.

Ivy stepped forward, flashing a smile. "Aunt Mildred. My friends here really wanted to get a sense of the atmosphere of this place, quietly look around on their own a bit, if that's okay. You and I can discuss the business aspects of bringing Aunt Mildred here. I've been through this with my own dear aunt, so I know the kinds of questions to ask." She waggled her fingers at Skylar and Trent. "You two go ahead. We'll catch up. I want to talk to Mrs. Cyr about the meals they provide."

The woman's face lit up. "Oh, we have wonderful cooks, even a head chef like you have at fancy restaurants. Our patients rave about how tasty everything is. And many of the staff eat their meals here too. The food's nutritious too, and catered to each patient's special needs."

"Of course," Ivy said. "May I meet the chef? Is he here?"

"Absolutely. They're prepping the dinner meal right now. And you can see that we have a beautiful dining area for those who are able to, and want to, take their meals here. We hand deliver to many of our patients who might not feel well enough for a cafeteria environment." Mrs. Cyr motioned for Ivy to follow her into the cafeteria.

Trent pulled Skylar with him down the hallway. He tried not to think about how good her hand felt in his and focused instead on keeping up the pretense of them being a married couple. "Finally. I thought we'd never get away from Mrs. Cyr."

Skylar laughed. "She's certainly attentive. I'm guessing that donation may have been a tad too large. She's been fawning all over us."

"Next time I'll have our guys cut the bribe in half. Does any of this look familiar or have they renovated and changed everything since you were here? It's under new management. When new people come in, they often change things, whether it's needed or not."

"It's different, for sure. New paint, new tile floor. But the layout, the bulletin boards listing activities, the soft music piping in through the speakers, even the fountain in the main lobby are very much like how I remember them. It's a relief, though, that the employees we've passed aren't the same people who used to work here. So far, I haven't seen anyone I recognize."

"Good. We won't stay long. Just walk me through your routine, literally and figuratively. Tell me what you used to do, take me where you used to go. Give me a feel for what it was like for you here. Did you speak to many people besides the patients you were here to visit?"

"Not much. Just check-ins at the front desk, really, and small-talk whenever I was in a room with a patient and one of the nurses or aids came in. For the most part I kept to myself, just me and the people I was coming to see." She motioned toward another hallway to their right. "This is the main area where I volunteered. Most people in this wing either aren't mobile or are too sick to leave their rooms. Those are the ones who request visitors the most. I met some wonderful people here. It's sad to think they're likely all gone now, unless they recovered and got better. It happens sometimes, but it's rare, at least in this section of the facility."

Trent led her down the hallway, going slowly to give her time to soak in the sights, the smells, anything that might trigger memories. He watched her smile sadly as they passed one room, touch her hand briefly to the closed door on another. It tugged at his heart that she obviously really cared about the people she'd visited, and that it still affected her years later.

He couldn't imagine purposely putting himself in that position, befriending and growing close to people knowing most would pass away soon. He was in awe of Skylar, knowing she willingly suffered that kind of pain because her desire to help others outweighed the high emotional cost to herself. Most people wouldn't, or couldn't, put themselves through that. Thank God there were people like her who did.

She tugged him to a halt just past one of the closed doors. "Why do you look so worried? Is something wrong?" She nervously glanced up and down the hallway.

He silently berated himself for not being more careful to keep his emotions hidden. “Everything’s fine. I was just wondering what you were remembering. Any details about the weeks and days leading up to your last day here could be important. Tell me who you visited, who you saw in that time frame.”

They continued their stroll down the long hallway as she told him about her routine, favorite patients, difficult ones too. When they reached the end of the hall, it opened up into a sitting area. There were several patients, most in wheelchairs, sitting in front of a large TV watching a movie. A few others were scattered around the large room on couches or recliners, chatting with each other.

“They seem so happy,” he said, as they headed to a couch against the far wall, away from the others.

“What did you expect?” she asked. “For everyone to sit around depressed?” She smiled. “That happens, of course. But most people I’ve met in hospice have faced their mortality and are ready to make the most of the time they have left. They’re at peace, enjoying their last days as much as possible. That’s what you see here, in this room. It’s the others, the ones who can’t leave their beds, who are the sad ones.”

“The types of patients that you visited.”

She nodded as they sat beside each other on a couch. “It’s sad that they’re fighting physical battles, unable to spend their time doing what they’d truly like to do. But you’d be amazed how much joy they still have the capacity to share if you hold their hand and listen.” Her face flushed. “I’m rambling. I’ve been talking your ear off.”

"Not at all. This is what I needed, to know what you did. You specifically mentioned three patients whom you got to know really well—Julius, Elsa and Martha. Were they the main ones you saw in the days before the shooting?"

She nodded, her hands clasped together, her knuckles whitening at his mention of the shooting. "Martha passed away a couple of weeks before…before I was last here. Julius passed a week after her. Elsa was holding her own, doing much better than the prognosis her doctors gave her. There was hope that she might recover enough to go home. Unfortunately, I never did find out what happened to her. I couldn't risk contacting anyone at that point."

"Were there any other memorable patients you didn't mention?"

"That I saw in the weeks before…I left?"

"Yes. We'll need to look into each of them, their families, due diligence to rule them out as being connected in any way to what happened." He pulled out his cell phone and opened a notes app.

"I can see you looking into the staff, like if there was some man who fixated on me for some reason. But the patients? That doesn't seem necessary."

He lowered his phone. "Tell me who shot at you then."

She blinked. "You know I don't know or we wouldn't be here."

"Exactly. We have no idea who's behind the attempts on your life. Which means everyone you came into contact with is a person of interest." He raised his phone again. "First and last names of anyone you even passed in the hall on a regular basis. Anyone you can think of."

She sighed. "Okay, okay."

She rattled off names, descriptions of how each person fit into her routine. Other than her patients, she didn't interact much with anyone else, as she'd said before. He was left with a small list. The top three were the patients she'd spoken the most about Julius Thompson, Elsa Norton and Martha Lancaster.

The Lancaster name made him pause. There was a prominent, wealthy family in Chattanooga with that name who bred champion Thoroughbreds both here and in Lexington, Kentucky. Skylar had said Martha's lawyer left her a large sum of money in an account after Martha passed away. It would make sense that if she was wealthy, she might have been related to the Lancasters famous for their horses. If so, could one of them have been angry about Martha giving away some of the family money? It seemed lame, given how wealthy the family was rumored to be. Certainly not incentive enough to go after someone for almost five years. But money made people do crazy things. He made a note to ask Callum to look into the infamous Lancasters to see whether Martha was a relation.

"There you are, dears." Mrs. Cyr beamed a smile at them as she hurried into the room.

A harried-looking Ivy rushed to keep up. Trent couldn't help but grin and immediately regretted it. The administrator's smile widened. Apparently, she thought his grin was aimed at her instead of Ivy.

"Mr. Adams have you been enjoying your tour so far?"

Since she was nearly trampling his feet, he couldn't even stand without risking pressing against her.

Ivy smirked at him but did nothing to facilitate a rescue as the administrator droned on about their cafeteria tour and recommended he come back some time so she could introduce him to the chef as well.

Skylar chuckled beside him as he struggled to keep up with the rapidly fired questions and information the administrator was throwing at him. He could well understand Ivy's exhausted look and he'd only been the focus of Mrs. Cyr's attention for a couple of minutes.

Taking mercy on him, Skylar stood and distracted the administrator long enough for Trent to sidestep her and get off the couch without causing either of them any embarrassment.

Tugging on his suit jacket, he stepped over to Ivy and spoke in a low tone. "You're going to pay for that."

"Oh, trust me," she whispered back. "You owe me far more than five uncomfortable minutes. That woman could give a sermon a preacher would envy. Nonstop talking. My ears are tired. Please tell me we're done here."

He glanced at Skylar, who looked as if she was ready to wave the white flag, since she was now the focus of the eager administrator expounding about the virtues of the hospice center.

"We're ready," he told Ivy. "Check with the team. Call me if there's any trouble outside."

"You got it." She hurried down the hallway before Mrs. Cyr could speak to her again.

Trent strode to Skylar, who grabbed his hand like a lifeline and let him pull her away. But even though he insisted to the administrator that they had to go, that they'd get back to her soon about their aunt Mildred, Mrs. Cyr chatted at them the entire way to the front lobby. It took another five minutes of thank-yous and forced smiles before they were able to escape out the front doors.

"That was torture," Skylar whispered as they hurried down the walkway outside. "I hope you got what you wanted from our fake tour."

He stopped her, just out of sight of the front doors. "Our tour isn't quite done. Now that we've walked the halls, hopefully things are more clear, the memories more focused. I need you to tell me about that very last day that you were here. Did it vary from your usual routine? Who did you visit?"

She pulled her hand free and clasped them together, something he noticed she did whenever she was anxious. "There was nothing unusual at all, nothing out of the ordinary. I got here at my normal time, my normal routine as you said. Martha and Julius had both recently passed. I hadn't picked up any new patients to visit yet. There was only Elsa."

"You didn't see anyone else? Speak to anyone on your way in or out? Meet anyone new or see someone you didn't recognize walking the halls?"

She shook her head. "I'm sure I spoke to the receptionist, Debbie… I can't remember her last name. Give me a minute. Let me think."

The receptionist's full name, Debbie Watkins, was in the police report that Trent had read. His people were already investigating her and anyone from back then that they could locate. But his hope was that Skylar might remember something she hadn't told the police. People who went through a traumatic experience as she had often thought of more details later, after they'd already spoken to the police. That's why follow-up interviews were so important. But that hadn't happened in her case, probably because there weren't any leads and the detective moved on to other cases, ones where someone had actually been hurt or killed. Lack of resources was a problem in law enforcement in general. It was why there were so many cold cases, and why Unfinished Business had more work than its investigators could ever get to.

"Don't worry about the receptionist's name," he told her. "It will come to you later. Was there anyone new that day? Unfamiliar?"

"No. No one. Oh, wait, I was wrong when I said I followed my usual routine. I arrived earlier than usual that Saturday. Normally, the staff prefers that you not come before lunchtime. That gives them time to feed, bathe, dress, and provide medications to the patients before dealing with visitors. But I didn't sleep well the night before and was up early doing weekend chores, so I finished earlier than normal. I decided to go to the hospice center early and see if they needed help with anything until Elsa was ready. Anyway, that's my long-winded way of explaining that I got here early. But I left at the same time as usual."

Trent made some notes in his phone. "That's good to know. If the shooter had planned to go after you on your way into the center, he might have gotten there too late and had to wait around for you to leave—or he left and came back. This many years later, though, I doubt we'll be able to find anyone who might have seen the guy lurking around waiting for you. But we can ask whatever staff we can locate from back then. When you left, you came out the front, like we did, right?"

"Yes."

"Did you see him then?"

"No, but I was probably fishing in my purse for my car keys as I walked."

"Walk with me. Think back and try to do what you would have done then."

"Seems silly, but here goes." She opened the purse Ivy had given her for this trip and dug around, pretending to look for keys, then pulled out a round makeup thing of some kind. He remembered her using it earlier to pat some color onto her cheeks. She clutched it in her hands. "I've got my keys, also known as my compact." She rolled her eyes, then started down the walkway. "My car was parked at the far end."

"Did you look toward the building, the woods to the left of it, toward the parking lot?"

She slowed, chewing her lip in thought. "I pretty much kept to myself on my trips here. I imagine I would have kept looking down at the sidewalk, or toward my car."

"And exactly where was your car?"

"You already know, from the police report."

"Humor me."

She pointed. "Last one in the row, not far from where your SUV is parked at the curb."

"You weren't looking toward the parking lot while you walked?"

"I don't think so. Like I said, I was probably looking down at the sidewalk, or my car. That's what I usually do."

They stopped a few feet from his vehicle.

"Why did you stop here?" he asked.

She frowned. "Because I stopped here that day."

"Why didn't you continue to your car? It was parked only twenty more feet away."

"I… I saw him. Across the street, near the trees. He was facing me, completely focused on me. It just felt… wrong."

"What did he look like?"

She shook her head. "Too far away for any real detail. I couldn't even guess his height without a frame of reference. It was January, cold. He wore a black trench coat and a black hat, the kind that pulls down over your head."

"Ski mask?"

"Something like that. It wasn't over his face, though. Just his hair, part of it. I did see some dark hair he didn't have covered. I could tell he was white, or at least, he had light-colored skin. That's it."

"That's a pretty good description for him to have been across the street. You did good."

"Yes, well, maybe the trauma of what happened burned his image into my brain."

"What happened next?"

"Instinct. Or training, really. Muscle memory from all the lessons my dad taught me about protecting myself. I trusted the bad feeling I got and dove to the side just as he brought up his gun and fired."

She ran her hands up and down her arms. "If I hadn't dived to the ground, I'm pretty sure that first shot would have gone right through my chest. I rolled, then jumped up and ran in a zigzag pattern to get behind the engine block of my car. He fired twice more, hitting my car, then…nothing. No, that's wrong. There were shouts. Other people coming out of the building. I think that scared him off. By the time I peeked over the hood of the car, he was gone."

"What about the white truck mentioned in police reports?"

"I remembered seeing the tail end of a white pickup going down the road after I peeked over the hood of my car. Since the man had disappeared, I thought maybe he was in the white truck. But I didn't get a license plate or a good description. No one did. And the police never found the truck, at least not one they could relate to what happened."

"You didn't actually see him get into the truck?"

"No."

"Maybe it wasn't his vehicle. Someone else was driving a truck and people assumed it was the shooter. The guy you saw could have come out of the woods, then ran back into them to get away."

"That's what the police said too. But there wasn't fresh snow to show any footprints. And the ground was frozen, hard, which made finding shoe impressions pretty much impossible."

"Did they use tracking dogs?"

"Not that I know of. Maybe they didn't see the point since I wasn't hurt, and there was no proof he was specifically aiming at me. Even I wasn't sure until the next attempt on my life. I couldn't see two incidents like that happening within a week or so of each other without them being related, and purposeful."

Trent leaned back against his SUV and crossed his

arms. "When you were walking, you said you were looking down, or maybe looking toward your car. Are you sure about that?"

She closed her eyes a moment. "As sure as I can be. I mean, that's the natural thing to do, look straight ahead as I'm walking along the sidewalk. I had no reason to turn and look anywhere else."

"But you did. If you hadn't, he would have hit you with that first shot. You said so yourself. Think back. Something made you look at him."

Again she closed her eyes, but a moment later she sighed in obvious frustration. "I don't know why I stopped and looked."

He pulled his keys out of his pocket. "Put the makeup thing in—"

"Compact." She smiled and dropped it into her purse.

"Hold these." He handed her his keys.

"Okay. Now what?"

He took her left hand and led her back toward the portico in front of the building. Once there, he turned her around facing his vehicle again. "This time, keep your eyes closed and hold my hand. I'll guide you while we walk. I won't let you fall off the curb."

"This is silly."

"Not if it leads us to the man trying to kill you."

Her eyes flew open and her gaze shot to his. Then she nodded and closed her eyes again. "Okay. I'm ready. What do you want me to do?"

"Feel the weight of the keys in your right hand. Remember that day. Let's walk, slowly. What do you smell?"

Her left hand clutched his as they moved down the sidewalk. "Pine trees. They're all over."

"Is that what you smelled that day?"

"Yes. Yes, but not as strong. It was cold. The air was crisp, clean."

"Keep walking. Listen. What do you hear?"

"Birds. Squirrels chattering."

"That day, what did you hear?"

She hesitated, then smiled, eyes still closed. "Same. Birds in the trees. Squirrels fussing because I was disturbing them. Maybe I was too close to their food supply. Wait. There was something else. The birds, loud, ugly squawking." Her eyes flew open. She turned toward the road. "Across the street. There were crows making a racket, flying out of the trees. That's why I stopped and turned. That's when I saw him."

"You heard the birds, turned and saw the man?"

"Yes."

"Had you ever heard crows out here before?"

"Not like that. They were loud, a grating noise. Very distinctive. That's what got my attention."

He stared at the woods a long minute. Then he made a signal in the air. Immediately, a man got out of a car in the parking lot and jogged toward them. Ivy headed toward them too.

"Wow," Skylar said. "I forgot they were here."

"There are more," he told her, as Ivy and the man joined them. "They're making sure no one suspicious gets anywhere near you."

"Is there a problem?" Ivy asked.

"Not a problem. I want to take a walk in those woods, check out where the shooter may have been standing, get his view of the parking lot. Will you guard Skylar? I want Ethan, our local here, to go with me since he knows the area."

"Sure thing. We'll wait in your SUV." Ivy held out her hand. "Keys."

"I've got them." Skylar handed them to Ivy. "But I'd rather go with you, Trent. I want to help."

"I appreciate that. But I can't guarantee your safety in the woods. Too many variables. Too many hiding places. I'll update you when I return. Won't be long."

He could tell she was disappointed, but she nodded and followed Ivy. He was relieved she wasn't insisting on going with him. He already had enough trouble focusing with her around. He didn't want to risk her safety any more than necessary.

"Ethan, let's head across the street."

They crossed the parking lot to the other side of the two-lane road out front. Ethan walked the tree line, scanning the ground, the scrub and pine trees as if he expected someone to jump out at them any second.

Trent thought about the police report, noted the distance to the parking lot entrance, moved a few more feet until he felt he was in the right spot—where the shooter had been standing that day. There was nothing remarkable about the location. Not that he'd expect to see signs of someone having been here this many years later. When he looked at the building, though, he could see why the shooter had chosen this position.

Ethan came up beside him, idly running a hand through his blond, spiky hair. "Smart choice. Slightly elevated. The cars wouldn't block his aim."

"Agreed. Perfect place for an ambush. Plenty of trees so he could blend in. No one coming out of the building would notice him right off." It shook Trent to realize that Skylar was right. If she hadn't ducked, she probably would have been killed. Even a poor marksman could have hit his target from here.

Ethan motioned behind them. "There's not what I'd call a trail anywhere that I saw. But there's a natural pathway between these trees like maybe there *used* to be a trail. The brush isn't too thick right here. Sure doesn't feel random that the shooter picked this specific place."

"He scouted it out ahead of time," Trent said.

"That's my take on it too. Cops didn't think so back then?"

"Since there wasn't an obvious motive, they leaned more toward carelessness than attempted murder. Didn't investigate it as thoroughly as they should have. Some people saw a white truck driving away right after the shooting. The police zeroed in on that, assumed the shooter was a hunter who took off right after it happened." He motioned toward the trees. "Show me that possible trail you saw."

About fifteen yards in, raucous shrieks sounded overhead. Birds squawked at them from the trees above. Crows, guarding their nesting area. Just like Skylar had described. It seemed likely the gunman had come through here. Which made it less likely that he'd hidden a vehicle somewhere down the road and ran to it after the shooting. Trent was betting he'd escaped into the woods.

"You're the local. If you were running through this section of woods, where would you go from here? What kind of topography surrounds this area?"

Ethan pointed off to the right. "Go south, you'll end up in some steep, rocky foothills with no way to go but up. Unless he brought climbing equipment, that'd be a dead-end. If you go north, you'll run into a house just out of sight of the hospice center. Nowhere to hide there since the lawn is cleared of trees. Risky too since someone might be at the house and see you."

"East then."

They continued through the woods for a good ten minutes. Trent was just about to call a halt, thinking they'd missed some kind of turn the shooter might have taken, when the line of trees abruptly ended. Stretching out in front of them was a white three-rail fence and rolling pastureland stretching to the horizon. Off to the right were a handful of horses grazing. They lifted their heads, curious about their visitors. But they quickly lost interest and went back to eating.

A small lean-to abutted the fence a few feet away housing two all-terrain four-wheelers. If someone started one of those up out here, this far away from the hospice center, would anyone hear them?

Probably not.

He waved toward the endless white fences and grazing horses. "Do you know who owns this property?"

"I couldn't swear to it," Ethan replied. "But I'm betting this land butts up on the far side to the Igou Gap Road area, or maybe Jenkins Road. It's all pricey homes and horse land over there. Given those expensive-looking Thoroughbreds, I'm pretty sure there's a big white mansion on the other side of that rise. Seems right. Yep, pretty sure."

"Who owns the mansion?" Trent asked.

"One of the wealthiest horse-breeding families in the tristate area. The Lancasters."

Lancaster. As in Martha Lancaster? What were the

odds that she'd be friends with Skylar, bequeath her a large sum of money, and then there'd be a direct path from the Lancasters' property to the site of an attempt on Skylar's life—without that attempt somehow being connected to the Lancaster family?

Of course, another equally plausible explanation was simply that Martha's family placed her in the nearest hospice center to their property so they could more easily visit her. There didn't have to be any nefarious reasons for their land to be in such close proximity to where Martha was, and thus Skylar.

But Skylar had said Martha's family almost never came to see her.

He pulled out his cell phone and made a call. "Ivy, is everything okay there? No issues?"

"All's well. Security has checked on us a few times. And before you ask, yes, the guard was one of the ones we vetted and met earlier. He's legit. Nothing else going on here but boredom and some rumbling stomachs wanting dinner. You coming back soon?"

"Actually, that's why I called. I need a favor."

Chapter Fourteen

Skylar woke with a start and sat up on the couch. It took a moment to get her bearings and figure out where she was—the family room of the two-story rental house on the outskirts of Chattanooga. She must have fallen asleep waiting for Trent to show up. Since the lights had been on the last she remembered, Ivy had probably turned them out and went upstairs to bed.

Was it midnight? Later than that? Maybe she should invest in a cell phone, or at least a watch, so she wouldn't have to rely on the stars to guess the time. The house was steeped in darkness, except for some moonlight shining in through the transoms above the windows.

And a sliver of light underneath the office door just past the staircase. Had someone broken in?

Goose bumps raised on her arms. She automatically reached for her backpack to get her gun, then swore. Her backpack was upstairs in her bedroom. Wait, she was overreacting. If someone had broken in, they would have set off the alarm. And Ivy would have been down here with her gun. Trent had asked her to do him the favor of taking her here, making sure she was safe until he arrived. And there was no reason for her not to trust Ivy.

She drew a slow, deep breath as her sleepy mind finally began to think logically. Trent. It must be Trent in the office. He'd finally gotten back from whatever errand he'd run. She rubbed her arms and drew another shaky breath. She was so tired of being afraid, of fearing the worst every time she heard a noise.

Or saw a light under a door

Living like this wasn't living. Trent had been right about that. She hoped that whatever he'd done tonight got them a step closer to ending the torture that her existence had become. If so, she wanted to know about it. She didn't want to wait even one more minute.

She padded across the thick rug in her bare feet, stopping when she caught sight of herself in a mirror above a decorative table. Maybe she should go upstairs and change before seeing him. She wasn't exactly indecent, but she didn't normally talk to men wearing her nightshirt. Then again, she'd kept her bra on just in case he came home when she was in the family room. And the shirt reached nearly to her knees. Ivy had done well buying her some clothes for this trip, but she'd misjudged a few things—like that Skylar was much shorter than her.

This was silly. The man had seen her in shorts before and the shirt covered more than they did. When she caught herself fussing with her hair, she rolled her eyes and knocked on the door.

"Come on in, Ivy," he called out.

She hesitated. Was he expecting Ivy? She turned to face the stairs, surprised she didn't see her there. Maybe she should go up and get her if Trent had an appointment with—

"Skylar?"

She whirled around, pressing a hand to her racing heart. "Trent. You, ah, surprised me."

His gaze dipped down, then quickly back up. He cleared his throat, then smiled. "You're definitely not Ivy."

There was a slight raspy quality to his voice that sent a flush of heat through her. *Stop it. He was expecting to see Ivy, not you.* "I can go get her for you if—"

"No, no. I didn't plan on updating her until morning. What are you doing up? Last I saw, you were asleep on the couch."

She blinked. "You saw me? Sleeping?"

He grinned again and leaned against the door frame, his long legs stretched out in front of him. "I did have that pleasure, yes, but I swear I only saw you for a second. As soon as I realized you were lying there, I went to my office to give you privacy. I'm not a voyeur."

She cleared her throat, not sure what to say. He'd had the *pleasure*? Of seeing her sleeping? If she didn't know better, she'd think he was flirting with her. *Was* he flirting with her? It had been so long since she'd had any kind of relationship, she wasn't even sure she knew what was involved anymore. And suddenly she wished she did. She missed people. She missed men. And of all the men she'd met in her life, Adam Trent was near the top of the most intriguing, handsome ones. Maybe the very top.

He frowned. "Skylar? I was teasing. You aren't upset are you?"

"Upset? No, no. Of course not. I'm just—I wanted to ask you, if it's okay, about what you were doing tonight. I mean, if it has to do with the investigation. If it's something personal, I certainly don't mean to pry. I, oh shoot. I'm sorry. You used to live here, in Chattanooga, with your...with... I'm sorry. You probably needed some time, space, to...reflect. Or whatever. I should have just gone to bed instead of bothering you. In fact, I'll shut up right now and head upstairs." She whirled around.

"Skylar, wait." He grabbed her shoulders, his touch firm but infinitely gentle as he pulled her to a stop and turned her to face him. "You've got nothing to apologize for. You're curious about the investigation. And I have something to talk to you about anyway. Some questions to ask. If you're up to it, I'll fill you in on what I've been doing."

"It's not...personal?"

He shook his head. "No. Come on in. Please." He pushed the door open wide and waited.

Not sure what to expect, she entered the office, then stopped in surprise. The room wasn't all that large. A desk sat in front of the window with one visitor's chair in front of it, and bookshelves ran along one wall. It was mostly neat, except for the top of the desk. Every inch was covered with papers and folders as if someone had turned on a fan and blown them all around.

"When did a hurricane hit Tennessee?"

He laughed. "Guess it is a bit of a mess. It's a lot of information to cull through and I was in a hurry to find what I needed."

"Did you? Find what you needed?" She stopped in front of the desk, trying to make sense of what she was seeing.

"I'm not sure yet. With any investigation, it's hard

to know what's a clue and what's not until everything almost magically comes together at some point. And I'm not at that point yet."

She picked up one of the pieces of paper, her eyes widening. "These look like police reports. Wait, John Lancaster? Any relation to Martha?"

"Husband. Or, he was. He died over ten years ago, well before Martha's decline."

"This looks like an arrest report. It's from twenty-one, no, twenty-two years ago. Why are you looking into Martha's deceased husband?"

He riffled through some of the papers, apparently looking for something. "Did you know Martha was the matriarch of a wealthy horse-breeding family? We're talking multimillionaires. Uber-wealthy."

"I knew she was well-off, but she didn't talk much about herself. She always steered our conversations toward current events, or asked questions about me."

He glanced up. "About you? Like what?"

She held her hands out in a helpless gesture. "Nothing and everything. She was a truly caring person, always wanting to know how I was doing, how my job was going. We talked about my dad, my mom, places I'd lived. Small talk, really. Typical stuff two friends would say to each other. Are you sure her family breeds horses? She never mentioned horses."

Nodding, he shuffled a few more piles of papers around. "There they are." He picked up a stack of photographs and sorted through them. "Here you go. Recognize her?" He set one of the pictures down on top of some papers at the edge of the desk.

She stared down at the picture of a smiling man and

woman on horses in the middle of a green pasture. Behind them were endless lines of white three-rail fences and what she could only call a mansion in the distance. It was just as bleached-white looking as the fences.

Pulling the visitor's chair close to the desk, she sat studying the photograph. "This is definitely Martha. No question. She was so young and vibrant here. You get used to seeing someone ravaged by disease and it's a shock to see them like this, healthy and happy. Is this her husband? John?"

"Fiancé, in that picture. But yes, that's John Lancaster. They were married for forty years before he died of a massive heart attack."

"She never mentioned a husband. I knew she was a widow, but she never talked about him."

"Did she talk about her children? Or her grandchild?"

She set the picture down. "Grandchild? She definitely never mentioned one."

"Randolph. He's still in high school. His parents are Richard and Phoebe. They must not be close either or I think she'd have mentioned him."

"She's not the only one who didn't volunteer information. You never answered my initial question. Why are you looking into Martha's dead husband? I can't imagine this is related to my case."

"Me either. And yet, here we are."

"I don't understand."

Holding the rest of the pictures in his hand like a deck of cards, he sat back. "You remembered hearing crows before someone shot at you. Something, or someone, had disturbed them before he fired the first bullet."

"Okay, and…?"

"When Ethan and I walked into those woods today, we disturbed some crows too. I remembered some birds return to the same nesting areas year after year. Later, I searched online and confirmed crows do the same thing. It's not a stretch to believe they've used that same nesting area for years. They're far enough back in the woods that it makes sense that the gunman probably passed through there on his way to try to kill you instead of him arriving in some vehicle, then driving away in the chaos without someone seeing him. If he hadn't gone through the woods, the crows wouldn't have put up a fuss until after the gunshots, not before."

"Meaning he relied on my routine, knowing when to expect me to come out of the building and got there just in time. That would explain why no one else saw him hanging around."

"Agreed," he said.

"Seems logical, including the crow part. But I'm still waiting to hear what that has to do with Martha."

"Patience."

"No one's ever accused me of being patient."

He grinned. "I'm definitely getting that vibe. Ethan and I followed a barely discernible path through the trees, but it was there. Probably hasn't been used in a long time but had been in the past. It ended at a horse pasture surrounded by white three-rail fencing. When I asked Ethan if he knew whose land it was, he said it belonged to the Lancaster family. And if we were to head up over the far hill, we'd be in the back yard of a white two-story mansion."

She slowly picked up the picture. "Like the one here? And those fences, are they the same?"

"They are." He pulled another photograph out from the stack and pitched it onto the middle of the desk. "That's a current picture of the Lancaster mansion. It's my theory that whoever shot at you came from the Lancaster property, through those woods, and escaped the same way. There's a shed of sorts out there with four-wheelers. I looked and saw the keys were in them, probably because the property is remote and they wouldn't expect someone to bother them. It's far enough away from the road that no one would hear them if someone started up the engine. The shooter could have driven one across the pasture and over the hill and disappeared long before the police got there."

"What you're saying is that the gunman probably used the Lancaster's property as an escape route and stole one of their four-wheelers to get away?"

"That's my theory, yes. It's why I went to the police station instead of driving you here this afternoon. I spoke to our Hamilton County liaison. He got me all of this, copies of files the police already had on the Lancaster family, including property records so I could verify the place I saw today really was theirs. I wanted to see if there was a police report about someone stealing a four-wheeler from them. There wasn't."

"Maybe the gunman ditched the four-wheeler on their property, so it wasn't really stolen. Once they found it, they didn't see the point of reporting it."

"Perhaps."

"You have another theory?"

"Not a theory so much as another possibility."

He sifted through the stack of pictures and pulled

out two. Leaning forward, he set them in front of her, side by side, facedown.

"We didn't get a chance today to visit the two other crime scenes where someone tried to run you off the road, and the gunman chased you into the Cherokee National Forest. But I reviewed the police report from the road incident. You saw the gunman better than at the hospice facility. He had dark brown hair, slightly curly. He was thin, had a light complexion. Did the man who went after you in the forest fit that description too?"

She slowly nodded. "I never got a really good look at his face, in any of the incidents. He was either too far away or I was too busy trying to get away. But, yes. The general description could fit all three attempts on my life here in Chattanooga."

He flipped both pictures over, revealing two similar-looking men.

She drew a sharp breath and pressed a hand to her mouth. Both of them fit the vision she'd carried in her head all these years of the man who'd tried to kill her. Her hands shook as she picked up the pictures and took a closer look. Then she set them down and wrapped her arms around her waist.

"Either of them could be the shooter, at least the one or ones here in Chattanooga who went after me. Who are they?"

"Richard and Scott. Brothers. Martha Lancaster's sons."

Chapter Fifteen

Trent tossed his napkin on top of his plate and set his coffee cup beside it. Across the breakfast table from him were Skylar and Ivy. Skylar was a bundle of nerves, moving her food around her plate but rarely eating any of it.

"If you don't like the waffle, I make a mean breakfast sandwich. The rental company stocked the kitchen with pretty much everything you could want."

"No, thanks. You already made exactly what I asked for, which is super cool by the way. I love a man who cooks."

He grinned and Ivy chuckled. Skylar's face flushed a light pink.

"Good to know," he said. "But obviously there's something wrong with my culinary skills today. You ate about two bites."

"It's not the food, believe me. I'm nervous. When is the video conference with your team going to start?"

Ivy stood and moved to the archway between the dining room and family room. "If that's a complaint that I took too long setting things up, you can blame Callum. I got everything on our end going long ago. He somehow managed to mess up the state-of-the-art equipment in our headquarters conference room. It took Brice over an hour to straighten it out."

"I can hear you talking about me," Callum called out through the speakers in the other room.

"Oh, good," Ivy called back. "Brice obviously hasn't let you touch the equipment again. The sound's still working."

Callum swore.

Ivy laughed and turned back toward Trent and Skylar. "The gang's all here, or there, I guess. On the TV. Ready when you are."

Trent arched a questioning brow at Skylar. "Ready?"

She pushed back her chair and stood. "I've been ready since the sun came up this morning. I'm dying to know what everyone has found out." She grimaced. "Bad choice of words."

Ivy headed into the family room. Trent circled the table and took Skylar's hands in his. "It's going to be okay. We'll do whatever it takes so you don't have to hide for the rest of your life."

She nodded, but didn't seem convinced. "Thank you. If nothing else, meeting all of you and getting to talk to people again has been wonderful. Helps me not feel invisible anymore."

The forlorn look on her face was his undoing. In spite of his determination to keep things professional between them, he couldn't resist the impulse to pull her into his arms and cradle her against his chest. And when she immediately put her arms around his waist and sank into his embrace, he didn't care that his team could see them through the archway via the camera that Ivy had clipped to the top of the TV.

Skylar mattered. And she needed to know she mattered, and that he cared what happened to her. His team needed to know that too. He wanted them to work their tails off on this case, no matter what it took. He wanted it solved and for Skylar to have a chance at being truly happy and safe.

A delicate clearing of someone's throat sounded from the other room. Ivy.

He sighed and stepped back, keeping his hands on Skylar's shoulders. "Ready?"

She smiled and let out a shaky breath. "Now I am. Thank you, Trent."

"Anytime."

Her face flushed a delightful pink again as they headed into the family room.

Ivy gave them a curious look, smiled, then moved from the couch to the occasional chair on the other side of the coffee table. It was a subtle statement, but loud and clear. She was making room for Trent and Skylar to sit beside each other.

They sat, with Ivy's gaze practically glued to them the whole time. His secret was definitely out, the secret he'd been trying to keep from himself as well. He cared about Skylar, more than an investigator's concern for his client.

The physical attraction had been instantaneous. He'd tried to ignore it and keep his emotions uninvolved. But the barriers he'd attempted to erect had fallen like dominos at an alarmingly fast rate. Having emotions tied up with a client was inconvenient, unprofessional and exceptionally risky. Dangerous. He should excuse himself from the case and put someone else in charge.

But he couldn't.

He had to see this through to the end. He'd just have to be careful and make sure he kept his thoughts clear, focused.

Somehow.

Concern was evident on Ivy's face, on his teams' faces as they watched him from the camera above the fireplace. He nodded, trying to silently reassure them that he had things under control, whether he did or not. Skylar, at least, didn't seem to understand the silence, the looks. She smiled gratefully at everyone, no doubt thinking their concern was for her, not for both of them.

He sighed, then smiled reassuringly at Skylar's questioning look and focused on the TV screen. "I appreciate everyone's help on this case."

"Me too," Skylar said. "Thank you all so much."

"Of course." Ivy told her. "That's what we're here for." She stared at Trent. "We're here to focus on our job, solve the case, help the client. That's what's important here. That's the only thing that matters right now. Isn't that right, Trent?"

He stiffened at her *un*subtle dig. "Of course. This case is definitely my core focus." He motioned toward the TV. "And even though each of you have cases of your own right now, you've been putting in extra time to help on mine. I appreciate it. Thank you all, and Ivy, especially, for coming down to help us out."

"I have to return to Gatlinburg after this call." Ivy gave them an apologetic look. "I have a meeting with a witness for one of my investigations. But if you need me to stay, I can try to make other arrangements."

"I'm sure I can handle things here without you," he said. "I've got the security company guys to help out as needed. But thanks. I do appreciate everything you've done, and your offer."

She gave him a tight smile, not entirely convinced. "Who starts this time? Brice? Callum?"

"I'll go first," Trent said. "I shared what I've been looking into already with Skylar. But I wanted to give all of you an update as well.

He proceeded to tell them about the trip to the hospice center yesterday, Skylar's recall about hearing the crows, then seeing the shooter. And finally, about following an old path that led to property he later confirmed was owned by the Lancasters. He explained his theory about the shooter maybe using that path and a four-wheeler to get away. And that both Scott and Richard, Martha's sons, fit the general description of the shooter, in all three incidents in Chattanooga.

Ivy shook her head. "That's weak. Half the men I know fit that description. And Skylar didn't get all that good a look at them, right?"

Skylar nodded. "Right. I didn't. I was too busy trying to survive. Since Trent showed me those pictures of Martha's sons, I've been going back and forth about whether they could be the guy I saw. I honestly don't know. I certainly couldn't pick them out of a lineup. And I still don't understand why they'd want to hurt me anyway. I visited Martha because she put her name on a list at the hospice center requesting that someone visit her. I never did anything bad to her. We were friends.

It doesn't make sense her sons would decide they hated me after she died."

"I have to agree with her," Brice chimed in from the Gatlinburg conference room. "There doesn't seem to be any true link there."

"Agreed," Trent said. "It's weak. Martha did give Skylar some money in her will. But the Lancasters are wealthy. That doesn't seem to be enough incentive to go after her if they were angry she got any money."

"How much are we talking about?" Ivy asked.

"Two hundred thousand," Skylar said.

Brice whistled. "That's a lot of money. Just how wealthy is this family?"

"Wealthy enough," Trent said, "that two hundred thousand is like petty cash. I went to the police station yesterday to see if they had any information on the Lancasters. More specifically, I wanted to see if they'd filed a stolen property report the day of the hospice shooting to support my theory that someone may have taken one of the four-wheelers to get away. No report was filed."

"That could mean no theft," Ivy said. "Which weakens your theory even more."

"Not necessarily. My theory holds that the shooter could have gotten away through the woods regardless of whether he was on foot or stole anything. The fact that there wasn't a report filed lends credence to the possibility that a Lancaster may have been the shooter—either Scott or Richard would be my guess."

Everyone started talking at once, speculating on the theory and pointing out more flaws in Trent's reasoning.

He held up his hand until they quieted down. "It's only been one day. I'm in no way convinced that the

Lancasters are involved. I'm just looking into the possibility that they could be so I can either rule them in or rule them out. As far as the information I received from Chattanooga PD, they have thick files on Martha and her sons. You were wondering how rich they were? They've got assets in the upper hundreds of millions. Not quite as well-off as our boss, but not too far away from that."

"Wow," Brice said. "The money Martha gave Skylar really is just a drop in the bucket. Doesn't sound like a motive for attempted murder going on five years now. Where do they get their money?"

"Most people think it's from their horse-breeding operation here and in Lexington, Kentucky," Trent said. "But the local police, and the FBI, have been investigating them for years, searching for links to organized crime. They've even followed them around to restaurants so they could pick up their used dishes and get DNA profiles, in case they could use that to connect them to any crimes. So far, they haven't gotten a hit. I remember hearing rumblings about that when I was a detective here. But nothing's ever been proven. If I find something else more promising, I'll jump on it. Brice, you were looking into Darius Williams—"

"Who's Darius Williams?" Skylar asked.

"That's my cue," Brice said. "He's the man who tried to kill you in the Smokies a few days ago. Although at nineteen, he was more a kid than a man. What a wasted life. Gatlinburg PD and Ranger McKenzie were able to put a solid background together on him before I began my own investigation. He was smart, made good grades, had potential to really make something of himself until his parents were killed and he was put in foster care. His foster parents seem like good, loving people. But as you can imagine, having his life upended like that was tough. He made poor choices, got mixed up with the wrong crowd, drugs, insert cliché here."

"Were you able to connect him to Chattanooga?" Trent asked.

"Not so far. And I don't think I will either. I spoke to some of his friends and the manager of his apartment complex, verified he was in Gatlinburg every day for the past two weeks. They were all quite forthcoming. Callum, you'll have to approve my reimbursement expense report since you're playing boss this week. Bribes aren't cheap."

Callum groaned. "On the bright side, maybe once Grayson sees our expenditures racking up, he'll decide not to put me in charge next time he and Ryland are both out of town."

"You wish." Brice laughed. "No one gets out of playing boss. It's a rite of passage."

Skylar touched Trent's shoulder and leaned in close. "I'm really feeling guilty about all these expenses, regardless of how wealthy your boss is. Keep track of what this is costing. I'll pay him back when I can. Somehow."

He shook his head. "Brice and Callum are teasing," he whispered back. "I promise Grayson won't worry about any of the expenses. Did you forget the part where he's a billionaire?" He squeezed her hand. "It's okay. Promise."

She nodded, but it was obvious the costs were bothering her. Which only reinforced his opinion about her good character. She was independent and didn't want to take advantage of anyone. He just wished he knew how to reassure her not to worry about the costs.

Grayson wasn't frivolous with his money. He was an intelligent and savvy businessman. But he'd known from the start that Unfinished Business wasn't a revenue maker, that it would take a lot of money to run the company. That was the cost of doing business, and he carefully groomed his revenue generating enterprises to generously fund the cold case investigations. No matter how outrageous or expensive an investigator's request for resources might seem, Grayson always did everything in his power to say yes.

Trent turned back toward the TV. "Brice, how can you be certain that Williams was in Gatlinburg, that he didn't leave town anytime recently?"

"Because with his criminal activities at night, a girlfriend, and his full-time job during the day doing maintenance at the apartment complex where he lived, he was almost too busy to sleep. Whoever hired him had to have come here, which makes sense since they apparently took him out when he failed in his mission. And I'm fairly certain he was hired the same day he went after Skylar. That morning he called in sick to work. If that pans out as when the mystery bad guy first made contact with him, you can use that timeline to help narrow down suspects there in Chattanooga."

"Right," Trent said, making a note on his phone. "Our bad guy would have been out of town most likely the whole day, first to hire a gunman, then to kill him to cover his tracks."

Beside him, Skylar shivered and rubbed her hands up and down her arms.

"Skylar, you don't have to sit here through any of this. I promise I'll update you when we're done."

"No, no, I'm okay. It's just…sad, and scary. And even though I've been living on the run for a long time, it's still overwhelming sometimes realizing someone wants me dead. They want me dead so badly that they've been tracking me down, over and over, and actually hired others to try to do the dirty work." She drew a shaky breath. "Please, go ahead. Continue with the meeting."

Part of him wanted to call a halt to the whole thing and convince her to wait in another room. He wanted to hold her and somehow chase her fears away too. But he also knew the best way to make her feel better was to solve this case, as quickly as possible.

"Anything else, Brice?"

"Not for now. I think Lance is ready to report on his investigation into the military angle."

"Hang on," Trent said. "I need to warn Skylar first."

"Warn me? About what?"

"I asked Lance, with Callum's help, to look into your father's past, including his military service. And before you get too upset, please understand the goal is to find out, if at all possible, why he was worried that someone might find him and your family. You said he created aliases for all of you and kept moving around, taught you self-defense and how to survive in the wilderness. He went to a lot of trouble to keep someone from ever finding him, and the rest of you. And here you are with someone after you. It's yet another coincidence that came up. And those are often red flags in an investigation so—"

She put her hand on his and smiled. "It's okay. I understand. It's jarring to think of anyone looking at my dad's past, especially since he was so private about it. But if you think it makes sense to do so, for my sake, I know he'd be okay with it. So I am too."

He nodded, relieved she wasn't upset. "Go ahead, Lance. Have you been able to find out anything useful?"

"Unfortunately, no. My contact isn't available and my own searches on Army Rangers in the time frame you gave me isn't coming up with anyone who seems as if they could be her father. I'll give him credit. He was good at covering his tracks, moving around, changing names. I've traced him and his family through the states and all the names and places they lived. But I couldn't tell you where he was born or where he lived when the family was overseas. I'll keep looking. I'm sure as soon as I can get in touch with my military intelligence contact, he'll have much better luck at getting me her father's real name. But until that happens, I'm setting this aside."

"Disappointing, but I totally get it," Trent said. "This one's hard. We don't have any DNA or fingerprints from any of the attempted murders. None of the usual shortcuts to help us zero in on a suspect. Skylar, think back to the attempts on your life after you left Chattanooga. Do you have any idea how your identity could have been revealed before each of those attempts? Had you done anything out of the norm in the weeks before?"

"Like what?"

"Go visit someone from your former life?"

"No. Never."

"Call them?"

"No."

"Send emails to anyone?"

"I don't even have an email address."

"What about social media accounts? I didn't find any under your name. Maybe you have one under one of your aliases?"

"I've never had a profile. When I searched for you online, it was through basic Internet searches with key words like the social media platform names. I didn't actually log onto any of them. I'm off the grid. No electronic trail. I pay for everything in cash."

"You said you stay at motels sometimes. You have to buy food, supplies, clothes, new shoes, books or whatever you use for entertainment. Even living off the land requires money. But your cash isn't in your backpack, not enough to live for years. You said you hide it when you go somewhere new. You carry that with you every time you change hide-outs?"

"Okay, no, not all of it. I do have a bank account. But it's not under the name Skylar Montgomery. It's under one of the aliases my father created a long time ago. And I rarely ever access it. When I do, I get enough money out at one time to last me for months."

"When's the last time you accessed it in relation to the latest attempt on your life?"

She frowned and thought back. Then her eyes widened and her face went pale. "About a week before."

He nodded, not surprised. "And the other attempts?"

"I don't know. If they were close to an ATM withdrawal, it never dawned on me at the time. I always assumed someone recognized me during one of my supply shopping trips in town from the old news reports from when I went missing. But even now, I'm not convinced that's how the bad guy found me. I've never done anything to connect that alias to my identity as Skylar Montgomery. No one knows about that except me."

"If I can interrupt here," Brice said. "It wasn't easy to figure out your alias and where you lived when you and your family were here in the states. And it took a network of resources most people don't have. Still, Callum and I made all the connections—in less than twenty-four hours."

As his words sank in, her face turned even more pale.

Brice continued. "The average guy on the street wouldn't have been able to do it nearly as quickly as we did. But my point is that it is doable. I connected all of your aliases to the Montgomery name."

She shook her head. "You'll have to explain to me some day how you did that. Because my dad was religious about keeping our aliases from connecting to each other. And in spite of what you just said, I still don't believe there's any way that you could have discovered the alias I've been using for my banking."

"What's the alias?" he asked. "If you don't mind sharing it with us."

"I don't see why not. My life's already in your hands. It's Julia Legrasse."

He blinked in surprise. "You're right. That one never came up in our searches."

"My dad created it specifically so I could use it in an emergency. He put a lot of money in the account so I'd have it if I ever did have to go on the run. I had never used it before all of this started years ago. There is no connection between that account and me as Skylar Montgomery."

"Somehow you have to be leaving an electronic trail or how else would the bad guys keep finding you?" Trent said. "Think about what you do when you go to a new town, or buy supplies. How about when you use computers, the Internet? You said you looked up Unfinished Business on the Internet in a motel business center. And you searched for information on me to decide whether you could trust me. What account did you use to do that?"

She smiled. "None. The searches were all conducted by logging onto the motel's guest network to access the Internet. And I logged on using the last name and room number of the guest who was checking in ahead of me. I didn't even use my alias. I didn't have to. I paid for my room in cash. And before you ask, no, I didn't provide ID. I convinced the registration clerk to forego ID, insisting I'd lost my wallet. The name I gave her was made up on the spot." She shrugged. "I don't even remember that name. I've never used it before, or since."

Trent shook his head. "Them finding you has to be related to your ATM withdrawals then. There isn't anything else you've said that explains it."

She held her hands out. "I'm sorry. I wish I could think of something else. But I've never figured out how they keep finding me. I've thought and thought and tried to—"

"Wait." Trent turned on the couch to face her. "What about the money that Martha Lancaster gave to you? You said it's in an account you can access if you ever need it."

"But I never have."

"What name is the account under?"

"My emergency alias, Julia Legrasse. But like I said,

I've never, not once, taken money out of it. And I don't transfer money from that account to the one my dad set up. Martha's money is just sitting there. Untouched. No electronic trail."

"Someone put the two hundred thousand in that account for you. Who did that?"

"Martha's lawyer. The only electronic link would be the one-time transfer from Martha's account to the one the lawyer created."

"Under your alias. It doesn't matter that you've never touched that account. Martha, and therefore her lawyer, knew you as Skylar Montgomery. And the lawyer also knew your alias since he set up an account under it for you to hold the money that Martha bequeathed you. He could have contacts in the banking industry. Every time you make a withdrawal under your alias, regardless of it not being the account you used for Martha's money, he could be getting notified."

Her eyes widened in dismay.

"I'll bet that's the connection," Ivy agreed. "He must be involved."

Skylar twisted her hands together in her lap. "I never thought of that. I trusted him because I trusted Martha. Even hearing you make that connection, it doesn't make sense. Why would a lawyer I'd never met before that want to kill me? And why would he be after me for almost five years?"

"That's what we're all going to work on finding out," Trent said.

Ivy nodded from her chair on the other side of the coffee table. "You bet we will. This is a great break, Skylar. What was the lawyer's name? Do you remember?"

The tension in her face smoothed out in an amused smile. "It's not a name I'd ever forget. Albert Capone."

Callum burst out laughing. "A lawyer named Al Capone? After the infamous crime boss in the 1920s? Now that's one for the record books."

"He made a point of telling me that the Al Capone mobster was named Alphonse, not Albert. And he told me to never, ever call him Al."

Callum laughed again.

Trent stared at her. "The lawyer who knew your alias was Albert Capone?"

Everyone on the call went silent and Skylar stiffened, which had him belatedly realizing his tone had come out harsher than he'd intended. But he'd been stunned when she said that name, a name he'd read in the police files on the Lancasters last night. But he'd never made a connection or considered it to be important.

Until now.

"Yes." Skylar's voice sounded defensive. "I didn't judge him by his name. He seemed like a decent person, certainly not someone I feared or ever thought would want to hurt me."

"I'm not blaming you. Forgive me that it sounded that way. I was just surprised you said that name." He glanced at Ivy, then at the TV screen at the others in the conference room. "We're back at ground zero again. The lawyer, Capone, isn't the one who sent hitmen after Skylar. He's dead. He died just a few weeks after Skylar left Chattanooga."

"How did he die?" Skylar's voice was shaking.

"He was murdered. Someone shot him."

Chapter Sixteen

Skylar carried the tray of food to Trent's office but stopped at the open door, shocked to see the mess inside. It was even worse than last night. The papers had spilled onto the floor all around the desk as if he'd swiped his hand across it.

She knew from seeing his home in Gatlinburg that he wasn't the messy sort. This case was really getting to him, evidenced by him standing at the window with his hands in his pockets. He was staring out at the gently sloping lawn and trees beyond. And he was obviously deep in thought and hadn't heard her.

She supposed it was a good thing that the case was bothering him. It had been bothering her for, well, it seemed like forever. The rest of her life depended on what he and his team could do in the next handful of days. That was scary on so many levels. But no more than what she'd already been through. Which was probably why she felt surprisingly calm right now.

"Trent? I made soup and sandwiches for us."

He turned, his gaze falling to the tray she was holding. He looked at his desk, then swore. "Sorry. For the language, and for the mess." He shoved papers to one side, clearing a spot.

"You certainly don't need to apologize for swearing or for your shockingly bad housekeeping habits," she teased as she set the tray down.

He smiled. "Funny how you can do that."

"Do what?" She raked some papers aside on the floor and pulled the guest chair over so she could sit.

"Make me smile. Even when that guy was shooting at us in the mountains, you made me laugh. That's a gift."

Her cheeks warmed. "Well, ah, thank you."

"You're welcome. Thank you. And thank you for lunch. I didn't realize it was getting that late."

"You've been cooped up in here ever since Ivy left for Gatlinburg and you told me to get out of your office."

He'd just taken a sip from one of the water bottles she'd brought and he coughed, covering his mouth. He cleared his throat. "I didn't order you out." He coughed again.

"You totally did. Not in those words, but when I wanted to brainstorm, or whatever, you said you didn't want my help."

"No. I distinctly remember saying I didn't *think* you could help, that I needed to sort through everything in my head."

"By yourself. Which is why I left you alone and watched some really boring TV for hours. With my hermit existence, I'm used to being alone, but I always had a good book to read. That's not the case in this place. Can you believe the owners don't have any books here?"

He gave her an exaggerated look of shock. "No. Really? Should I call the police and report them?"

"Eat your lunch."

He laughed and reached for one of the plates.

As they ate, she skimmed some of the papers on the desk and asked him questions. In turn, he asked her about her life in the woods and isolated motels. They spoke about when someone shot at her car and tried to force her off the road. And they discussed what little she remembered of her feverish wanderings in the Cherokee National Forest when the wound in her side became infected. She told him about her father's survivalist training, how she drew on that training to know how to find water, what berries were edible and which ones would kill her.

He wiped his mouth with his napkin and sat back, shaking his head. "Your father sounds like an amazing man. I wish I could have met him."

She crossed her arms. "You would have admired each other, I think."

"How did he die? Brice didn't mention anything nefarious happening to him when he updated us on his investigation."

"Nefarious. Interesting choice of words. I'd say it was nefarious that a drunk driver T-boned my dad's car. He had one of those older models without side air bags. He died instantly."

He reached across the desk and took her hand. "I'm so sorry. You were in college, right?"

She latched on to his hand, not even caring that she probably seemed desperate. Feeling his skin against hers warmed her heart like nothing else. It calmed her and helped ease the pain. He said she had a gift to make him laugh. His gift was that he could take away her fears, her grief, make her feel better just by touching her.

"Are you okay? I didn't mean to make you sad." He gently rubbed his thumb across the backs of her fingers.

"I'm okay. You didn't. I mean, you did, but you made me feel better too." Since she was thinking about tugging him closer, she forced herself to let go of his hand and sit back.

"I was a sophomore in college when the accident happened. Mom had died of cancer years earlier. For the first time in my life I was all alone, no family of any kind. And the life my dad lived, always on the move, teaching me to keep others at a distance, meant I didn't have any close friends. That's partly why I decided to transfer to the University of Tennessee here in Chattanooga. I was hoping to find some relatives on my mother's side. But I never did."

He sat forward and rested his forearms on top of the desk. "You mentioned that before, about trying to find family here. Can you give me more details?"

"There's nothing to tell, really. I heard my mom on the phone sometimes through the years talking to people I thought might have been family. I heard her say something about Chattanooga a couple of times and guessed that maybe she was from here. But whenever I asked her about it, she went silent, refused to talk about it. Usually, after one of those phone calls, Dad would give us new names and we'd relocate. I could tell my father was upset. But he never yelled at my mom. I got the impression that he understood how lonely she was for people in her past. He understood why she broke the rules. But it made things tough, us having to move so often."

"You don't have any idea what your mom's maiden name might be?"

"I really don't."

"And she wasn't afraid of whoever she spoke to on the phone? She got along well with the people from her past?"

"Oh goodness, yes. She was happy when she was on the phone. Why would you ask that?"

"What you've said is more evidence that it's your father who had a reason to run, not your mom. Whoever was trying to find you was after your dad. And if Chattanooga was her hometown, it's likely your father lived here too. At least long enough to form a relationship with her."

"I suppose. Does that help us?"

"It's another puzzle piece." He pulled out his cell phone and started typing a text. "I'll pass that along to Brice in case it helps him with his research. He can make an assumption that your father joined the Army when he lived in Chattanooga. It's another piece of data that might make things click when he speaks to his military contact. It could help us get your father's real name. From there, we can try to find out who his enemies were and why he was worried about being found."

"You still think that whoever was after him is the same person who's after me?"

He stared at her, his brows wrinkling in concentration.

Feeling self-conscious, she glanced down to make

sure she didn't have any food on her blouse or a button undone. "What is it? Is something wrong?"

He blinked as if just realizing he was looking at her. "No. Not at all. Just thinking about what you said. How old are you?"

"Never ask a woman her age." She smiled.

"It's important. I'm guessing… Well, I won't guess."

"Smart man. I'm in my early thirties. And that's as specific as I plan to get."

He chuckled. "Fair enough. You said your father left the military when you were a little girl. So whoever was after him started decades ago. Do I think the exact same person is after *you* now, this much later? Not likely. Too much time has passed. I'm still convinced there's a connection, though. Which means whoever is after you is likely related to the person who was after your father, or at least close friends of the family. Someone who feels wronged."

"You think it's a family vendetta? That the grandfather went after my dad. And when that didn't work out, maybe after the grandfather died, his son decided to go after me?"

"Something like that. Possibly. Again, it's only a theory." He stood and put their dishes on the tray. "I'll take this to the kitchen. I need to call Brice and talk some of this through. Be back in a few minutes."

After he left, she stood and crossed to the window behind the desk. Looking out at the trees and rolling hills surrounding this remote property should have calmed her. But talking about her mother had dredged up feelings she usually shut away deep in her heart. To her dismay, hot tears coursed down her cheeks. She drew a shaky breath, and another, trying to move past the pain, to lock the memories back up where they didn't have the power to hurt her.

Instead, the tears fell harder and she let out a little sob. She clenched her fists and pressed her forehead to the cool glass, her shoulders shaking as more sobs came no matter how hard she tried to stop crying.

Suddenly, Trent's arms were around her, turning her and pulling her against his chest. She clung to him as he drew her close.

"It's okay," he whispered, resting his cheek against the top of her head. "It's okay. I promise. Everything will be all right."

His empathy and gentle strength, his understanding released the floodgates and she cried even harder. He rubbed a hand up and down her back, whispering soothing words as he patiently held her through her crying jag.

Finally, when the tears slowed, she sighed raggedly, her face still cradled against his chest. "I miss them. I miss them so much."

His hand continued its slow, soothing caress up and down her back. "Your mom and dad?"

She nodded. "It's been years. Most of the time I can think about them and smile, even laugh. But sometimes, it hits so hard, as if it only just happened."

"Grief is like that," he whispered, then gently kissed the top of her head. "It comes in waves, never really going away."

She pulled back to look up at him, her arms still around his waist, his arms still holding her close. "I'm so sorry about your wife. I could tell when you mentioned her before that you loved her very much."

"I did. I do. Always will."

"How long were you married? If you don't mind me asking?"

"I don't mind. Just a couple of years. But we dated for a few years before that." He gently feathered her bangs out of her eyes. "You're nothing like her. And yet, you're very much like her. She was quiet, timid at times. Guns terrified her. But she was smart, strong, generous."

"She sounds perfect."

He smiled. "You sound jealous."

"Ha. You wish."

He laughed. "Better now?"

She sensed he was about to pull away, but she wasn't ready, so she tightened her arms around him. "Thank you, Trent. Thank you for always being there for me. No one else has been, for so long. And even though we've only known each other a short time, it's crazy but it feels like I've known you forever. I hope we'll always be friends, even when this is over, however it turns out."

On impulse, she stood on tiptoe and kissed his cheek. But as she stepped back, he gently slid his hands into her hair, framing her face, and stared down at her.

"I want to kiss you," he whispered, sounding frustrated. "Really kiss you."

"What's stopping you?"

He grinned. "See? You always make me smile. Even when I'm struggling between what I *should* do and what I really, really *want* to do. I need to stay professional, focused. This isn't right." Even as he said it, his thumb brushed against her mouth.

She shuddered with pleasure and slid her arms up his hard chest.

His Adam's apple bobbed in his throat. "Skylar, we shouldn't—"

"I don't know who made these silly rules. But I never agreed to them."

He laughed. "You're really something, you know that?"

"So you've told me. But I'd rather be kissing than talking."

He groaned. "I'm going to regret this."

"I'm not."

He was laughing when his lips touched hers. Then everything turned serious. She'd been kissed before, but never like this. The world around them melted away. It was just the two of them. Nothing else mattered. Nothing else existed.

He moved his mouth against hers like a master, making her moan deep in her throat. His tongue caressed her lips, then stroked against hers in a mating dance that had her belly tightening. All she wanted was to get closer, to feel his skin against hers, his hard planes against her soft curves. She stood on tiptoe, trying to loop her hands behind his neck, groaning in frustration when she couldn't reach.

Instinctively knowing what she wanted, he picked her up, supporting her bottom with one arm as he turned and sat on top of the desk without breaking their heated kiss. She was on his lap, her breasts crushed against his chest, her legs curled around his waist. His kiss turned ravenous, drinking her in, making her toes curl inside her shoes.

Hot, so hot. So very, very good. She slid her hands

down his chest to the buttons of his shirt and popped the first one open.

He broke the kiss, gasping for breath, his forehead against hers. “We have to stop.”

She opened another button and slid a hand inside across his pecs.

He shuddered and grabbed her hand. “Skylar—”

“I want this, Trent. I want you.”

He groaned and captured her mouth with his again. But when she tried to undo another button, he grabbed her roving hands in his, stopping her. He drew back, pressed another quick kiss against her lips, then lifted her and set her on the chair in front of the desk.

“Trent—”

“Shh. Give me a minute.” His voice was thick and raspy. He seemed to be struggling to get himself under control.

She curled her fingers against her palms to keep from reaching for him again, even though she desperately wanted to. But no means no. He wanted to stop. She had to honor that, even if she didn’t understand it.

A minute later, he let out a deep breath, then got down on his knees in front of her chair, which made them eye level. His gaze dropped to her lips and he swallowed, then shook his head.

“You’re dangerous.”

She grinned. “What a sweet thing to say.”

He laughed and shook his head again. “What am I going to do with you?”

“Anything you want.” She waggled her brows.

He was still laughing when he stood and drew her up to stand in front of him. “I’m more than glad to know that I'm not the only one struggling against an attraction here. But we really do need to focus on the investigation. I need to concentrate on keeping you safe and that means no distractions."

"Now I'm a distraction?"

He took her hands in his. "You are so much more than a distraction, Skylar. You're sexy as hell. But more than that, you're important to me. You matter."

She laced her fingers with his. "You matter to me too. Why do you sound so doom and gloom about it?"

"Because it's unprofessional, for one. Having a personal relationship with a client crosses a line I never intended to cross. Emotions are heightened during times of trauma and stress like what you're going through. You could misread your feelings, regret this later when you're thinking more clearly. I'd be taking advantage of you to allow this to continue." He tugged his hands free and started rebuttoning his shirt.

"I don't understand any of that. And I sure don't agree with it," she said.

He gently tipped up her chin. "If the way you think you feel about me right now is real, those feelings will still be there after the investigation is over."

"So you're not dumping me before we even really get started. You're just…postponing?"

He kissed her forehead, then pulled back, smiling. "I'm most definitely not dumping you."

"Well, okay then. If you're not going to let me jump your bones, what do we do now?"

He burst out laughing, then pressed a quick kiss against her lips before pulling away. "I need to go see Capone's old business partner, James Mattly. He's the other lawyer from Capone's practice. I made an appointment to see him in—" he pulled out his cell phone "—about forty-five minutes. I want to find out what Capone was doing before he was killed almost five years ago."

"Ever notice how often that time frame of five years comes up?"

"I've definitely noticed. Something else I've noticed is that the attacks on you have heated up recently. There've been more this past year than the other five put together."

She blinked. "You're right. There's been an escalation. You think there's some kind of time frame involved?"

"It's possible. That's what I'm hoping to find out from Mattly. Maybe there's a deadline associated with hitting the exact five-year mark."

"Five years from what, though? From the first attempt on my life?"

"Maybe, or something close to it."

"Martha died almost five years ago. If this is related to the Lancasters, could that be the date?"

"It's crossed my mind. The anniversary of her death comes up next week."

She nodded. "We've only got a handful of days until..." She shrugged. "We don't even know what to worry about, if indeed there is an anniversary involved."

"I don't want you worrying about anything. Which is why I'm going to get a couple of the security company guys over here before I leave for my meeting." He rounded the desk and pulled open a drawer. "I've got Ethan's business card in here with his number, so I'll—"

"No." She stood. "I'm not staying with Ethan. I'm going with you."

"Skylar, that's not happening. It's too dangerous."

"Why? Are you worried that Mattly's taken up where Capone left off? That he's the one trying to kill me?"

"It's a potential theory, yes."

"It's a dumb theory. Martha is the one who hired Capone specifically because she cared about me and wanted to give me money. Trust me, if he was hired by Martha, he had nothing to do with her sons. She couldn't stand her sons."

"That's news to me. I haven't heard any hints of that over the years. There's certainly no mention of it in the police files."

"It's true. She talked about them a lot, about how they used her for her money and never came to see her unless they wanted something. They weren't close. She felt they couldn't wait until she died so they could get her money, even though they're both wealthy in their own right from the inheritance their father left them. But where they got millions, Martha got hundreds of millions. She said the money destroyed her family and she wished they'd never been rich in the first place. So, you see, she wouldn't have hired a lawyer who was friendly with her sons. So if you truly think Scott or Richard Lancaster are behind everything, we have nothing to risk by going to see Capone's old legal partner," she reasoned.

"What if you're wrong? What if it has nothing to do with the Lancaster brothers and everything to do with Martha's lawyer, and by default, the lawyer's old partner?"

"I think you're reaching. But if that's the situation, then what better way to flush him out than to have me show up?"

"You're suggesting I use you as bait?" His voice was clipped, angry.

"No. I'm suggesting that *I* use me as bait. I'm a grown woman. I understand what's at stake and I'm willing to take that chance."

He yanked the drawer open and fumbled around inside. "Forget it. I'm not risking your life. I'll call Ethan."

"You risked my life the moment you drove me to Chattanooga."

His head shot up. "That's not fair. The last attempt on your life was in Gatlinburg. I couldn't leave you there. It made more sense to take you with me, jog your memories, shake loose some leads in the investigation."

"It was still a risk. Someone could recognize me."

He pitched a business card on top of his desk and shoved the drawer closed. "The odds of that are exceedingly low. Your makeover was precisely so we could keep your identity secret. You look nothing like you did back then."

"I'm glad you feel that way. That means I can go with you to see Mattly. He won't recognize me." She smiled and crossed her arms.

He narrowed his eyes. "I walked right into that one, didn't I?"

"Yep. How far away is his office? We should probably leave soon. You're in a suit. Should I wear a dress for our appointment with a lawyer? Ivy brought me a few nice ones."

"I haven't said yes."

“You could make it safe for me. I can bring my gun too. Just in case.”

“No gun. Forget it. You’re not coming with me anyway.”

“And when we leave,” she continued, “you can drive all the two-laners you want until you’re certain no one is following us.”

He rolled his eyes, a reluctant grin tugging at the corner of his mouth.

“Have I mentioned I’m really stubborn?” she asked.

“It wasn’t necessary. There’s a neon sign over your head and it’s flashing.”

“Great. When do we leave?”

Chapter Seventeen

James Mattly's law office was in a seedy part of town on the second floor of a rundown-looking two-story wooden building. The parking spaces were right off the two-lane street, facing the curb. All of them were empty except one, which Trent guessed belonged to Mattly. The car was a Mercedes, but the name was the only thing prestigious about it. It had to be at least fifteen years old. The silver paint was flaking off. And the rear bumper had dents all over it, likely from cars driving down the narrow street and clipping it.

Trent debated the wisdom of parking his SUV there, but he didn't have a choice unless he wanted to walk several blocks. That would be too far to give Skylar and him a quick escape if things went bad. Her heels would slow her down and put her at risk for a fall if she had to run that far.

He chose the spot on the far side of the beat-up Mercedes, hoping it would shield his vehicle from any bumper mishaps.

Beside him, Skylar opened the glove box and pulled out her pistol.

Trent swore and grabbed it. "What are you doing

with that? How did you even sneak it in here without me noticing?"

She rolled her eyes. "It wasn't that difficult. And I'm checking the magazine to make sure you didn't switch it out again. I don't want to get in a gunfight with no ammunition."

He leaned past her and shoved her pistol in the glove box, then locked it. "I have no intention of getting into a gunfight."

"That's the thing about gunfights. They're never planned. Do you have *your* gun?"

"Of course. I told you. I'm always carrying."

"Then why can't I have mine? I can probably shoot better than you."

"Without a doubt. I've seen you shoot. But you don't have a concealed carry permit. If, God forbid, things go crooked, I don't want the police locking you up for having a gun illegally."

"You don't have a permit either, not under your alias, *Mr. Adams*."

"I do, actually. That's one of the things Brice created for me, along with my ID."

"That's not fair. He should have given me one."

"Next time people are trying to kill you and we need fake IDs, I'll be sure to get you a gun permit."

"Now you're making fun of me."

"I wouldn't dare," he teased. "As for me being Mr. Adams, not for this meeting. Our names are Mr. and Mrs. Palmer. Don't volunteer anything about yourself. If he asks you a question, I'll answer."

"Why aren't we using the aliases that Brice made for us?"

"Because if Mattly's one of the bad guys, I don't want him figuring out there's a rental on the outskirts of town under the names of Mr. and Mrs. Adams."

"How would he figure that out?"

"The same way the bad guy kept figuring out where you were. He'd use his contacts to look for an electronic trail. In this case, we have the lease, including a deposit made via the Adams alias. Using an alias for the rental kept our real names secret. Having the ID and paperwork to match is just in case questions come up about the rental and whether we're the legitimate renters. At the hospice center, we needed ID to sign in. No getting around it, so we used the Adams alias there too. But the security company we hired vetted the staff, confirming no one worked there who had when it was under different management five years ago."

"Got it. In this case, with the lawyer, we don't know enough about him to feel safe risking a connection to our electronic trail under Adams. Thus, we're now the Palmers. Makes sense." She held out her hand. "May I see your concealed carry permit under the Palmer alias?"

He gave her an aggravated look. "This is fun for you, isn't it?"

She grinned. "It kind of is, actually."

"You do realize this is deadly serious, right? If Mattly is the one who killed Capone, he could be in cahoots with whoever's mixed up in all of this."

"*Cahoots?* Do people actually use that word in this century?"

He clenched his jaw. It was either that or start yelling. Or kiss her. And where had that thought come from?

Of all the times for him to need to stay focused, this was it. After a few deep breaths, he popped the door open and got out.

An only slightly apologetic-looking Skylar accompanied him inside the building. On the second floor landing, he paused outside the door to *Mattly Law Offices* and looked back at her.

"We're Mr. and Mrs. Palmer," he reminded her, keeping his voice low. "Stay close to me and don't get near him. I mean it, Skylar. I don't want something bad to happen to you. I already regret letting you talk me into this."

She nodded gravely. "Thank you for caring about me. I'll be good. Scout's honor."

"You were a Girl Scout?"

"Heck no."

He laughed. He couldn't help it.

She put her hand on his to stop him from opening the door. "I *am* taking this seriously in spite of how it might seem. I'm just not 'doom and gloom' right now, which is nice for a change. It feels as if a weight's been lifted off my shoulders because I feel somewhat in control of my own destiny again. I deeply appreciate you giving me a chance to fight for myself instead of making me hide at the house."

He sighed and nodded. "I understand."

Then, as if he hadn't just given himself a silent lecture about being focused, he kissed her. It was a quick kiss, barely even qualified as one. And he regretted it as soon as he did it. All it had done was make him long to kiss her again, really kiss her, and run his hands across her— He cleared his throat, straightening while mentally berating himself for being so weak. Then he noticed how rattled she looked and couldn't help grinning. Maybe he should kiss her more often, if only to distract her. The problem was that it distracted him too.

Focus, Trent. Be professional.

Gently pushing her behind him, he opened the door and led the way inside.

A grizzled-looking older man in a rumpled gray suit looked up from his desk. It was piled so high with stacks of folders and papers that he had to look around one to see them. More stacks were in two-foot-high rows along every wall. A couple of scarred wooden chairs sat in front of the desk facing a tattered love seat.

He smiled in greeting. "Mr. and Mrs. Palmer?"

Trent nodded and strode forward, holding out his hand. "Mr. Mattly, thanks for seeing us on short notice."

They shook hands and Mattly waved them toward the love seat. "Sorry about all the paperwork lying around." He sat across from them on one of the wooden chairs. "I'd say it's filing day as an excuse for the mess, but I'd be lying. I ran out of storage space years ago." He shrugged. "You make do with what you have. Now, how can I help? You said on the phone it was urgent." He smiled and nodded at Skylar.

Trent leaned forward, purposely drawing the lawyer's attention away from her. "I'll get right to the point. An acquaintance of ours was a friend of Martha Lancaster's. As I'm sure you know, Martha passed away several years ago. She was a client of your partner's, Albert Capone. There have been some complications for our friend since Martha's death that we believe may be linked to whatever Mr. Capone was doing on Martha's behalf."

Mattly held up his hand to stop him. "Mr. Palmer, Mrs. Palmer, you have my sympathies about whatever these complications may be. But I'm confused as to why you're telling me this."

"Since Martha was your firm's client, I wanted to ask you some questions about the work done for her. It might help me figure out why someone is harassing our friend."

"I'm truly sorry that someone is bothering her. But the police are the proper authorities to speak to about that, not me. I'm not sure who led you to believe that I could offer any information about Mrs. Lancaster. But I assure you, there is absolutely no connection between her and this firm. She has never been a client of mine, not that I would share information if she were. It would be unethical. I truly can't help you."

Trent studied Mattly's expression, his mannerisms. For the most part, he didn't seem to be paying much attention to Skylar. And he didn't seem to have recognized her, which was encouraging. The vibe he was putting out was that of an honest, struggling lawyer, not a criminal mastermind or a hitman.

"Mr. Mattly, that's semantics. Saying Martha was never *your* client isn't the same as saying she wasn't a client of the firm, courtesy of your partner. We already know she was Mr. Capone's client. And since your partner passed away, you should now have possession of his files. That's why we came to you."

Mattly crossed his arms.

Trent tried again. "He drew up her will. You have to be aware of that, at least."

Mattly continued to give him the silent treatment.

"I just want to know whether he did anything else on her behalf that could help explain why someone is bothering our friend. It all began shortly after Mrs. Lancaster's death, close to the time that Mr. Capone was killed. It's in both of our interests to look into your file on Mrs. Lancaster. It could hold clues about our friend and who killed your partner."

His face turned a mottled red. "This is all highly inappropriate. Unless you're a police officer, with a warrant, I'm certainly not showing you anything."

"I'm interpreting that as meaning you do have the file I'm interested in. You're just not inclined to let me look at it, in spite of what I just said. Why not? It won't hurt anyone and it has the potential to help a great deal, including perhaps solving your partner's murder."

"You need to leave, Mr. Palmer." Mattly headed back to his desk. "If my partner worked with Mrs. Lancaster, and I'm not saying he did, attorney-client privilege prevents me from disclosing that."

Trent stood to see him over the stacks of folders and papers. "Both the client and her attorney have passed away. Attorney-client privilege no longer applies."

"So you're a lawyer now, in addition to being a, what, private investigator? Please don't lie and say you're not. It's rather obvious." He motioned toward the door. "Again, I'd appreciate it if you would get out of my office."

"You're right." Skylar stood and approached the desk.

Trent grabbed her arm and anchored her to his side. "Honey, what are you doing?"

She ignored him and kept her gaze locked on the lawyer. "My husband is an investigator, that's true. But his goal is to save my life, not this nonexistent friend he referred to. We're here because Martha was a dear friend of mine and we know that she wouldn't have wanted any harm to come to me because of her bequeathing me some money. And I know that Mr. Capone drew up her will because I met with him. He came to the hospice center to speak to both Martha and me."

Trent swore. "We're leaving." He tugged her toward the door in spite of her trying to pull her arm free.

"Wait," Mattly called out. "Please."

As they approached the door, Trent looked back to see Mattly hurrying toward them. Trent turned to face him as he pushed Skylar behind him, then flipped back his suit jacket, revealing his holster.

"Don't come any closer, Mr. Mattly."

Mattly stopped and held his hands up, his eyes widening. "Good grief. You really are concerned about your wife's safety, aren't you?"

"We didn't come here for fun, that's for sure."

Mattly let out a shaky breath and slowly lowered his hands. "Okay, okay. Yes, it's true that Albert drew up a will for Mrs. Lancaster. I don't know the details. I didn't assist him with it and had no reason to read it. Any files he had on her I immediately destroyed after his death."

"You expect me to believe that?" Trent motioned toward the stacks of paperwork all over the office. "You probably still have the files from your very first client in here."

Mattly grimaced. "You wouldn't be wrong. My wife won't even come here because the mess drives her to distraction. But in this case, I swear I didn't hold on to the file. I destroyed it, just like I told you. I wanted nothing to do with it."

"Did you go through the files from his other clients to see if what he was working on for them could have led to his murder?"

"Of course I did."

"But not the Lancaster file."

"No. Absolutely not." He sighed and rubbed his eyes. "I honestly, swear to God, do not know what was in it. I didn't want to know, even if it would have solved Albert's murder. Some things are better left alone. I'm not talking out of school to say what everyone who's ever met Martha's sons knows. They aren't the kind of men you want to cross. I warned Albert not to take Martha on as a client. But he didn't listen."

"You believe that one or both of her sons killed your partner."

He glanced toward the windows as if fearful that someone outside could hear him in his second-floor office. "I didn't say that."

Obviously, Mattly was too intimidated by the Lancasters to talk. There wasn't any point in pushing him anymore.

"I guess we're at an impasse. We'll go. Thank you for your time."

"Mr. Palmer?"

Trent arched a brow in question.

"Whatever you're really after, I beg you to remember that my partner got on the wrong side of the Lancaster brothers. Now he's dead. Be careful. Be very, very careful." He started to close the door, but Trent pushed his hand against it, stopping him.

"What exactly did your partner do to get on their wrong side?"

"I would think that's obvious. They didn't want him to file the will." His eyes took on a faraway look. "Albert was a good man. Ethical. Stubborn. He didn't take kindly to threats. And he felt strongly that Mrs. Lancaster should get to determine how the courts divided up her estate regardless of her son's wishes. He ignored their warnings and filed the will. A few hours later, he was dead."

Chapter Eighteen

Trent flipped the dead bolt after he and Skylar entered their rental house from the garage.

"I'll be in the office reading more of those police files." He strode past her into the family room.

"And I'm going to change into some jeans to get comfy. Trent?"

He stopped, silently praying for patience before turning and arching a brow in question.

"You haven't said a word since we left the lawyer's office. I know you're disappointed that we didn't get the information we'd hoped for. But we met Capone's partner and got a good sense of the kind of person he is. I'm guessing he's not on your suspect list anymore. That's progress, right?"

He stiffly nodded.

"So what's got you upset?"

He stared at her incredulously. *"What's got me upset?"* He strode back to her and stopped a few feet away, forcing her to crane her head back to meet his gaze. "I asked you not to tell Mattly anything. You proceeded to tell him that you met Capone at the hospice center and that Martha bequeathed you money. Even a simpleton can connect those dots after reading the will. Mattly may seem like an okay guy. But he's terrified of the Lancaster brothers. If they lean on him for information, I doubt it would take him long to crack under the pressure. You might as well have called the brothers yourself and told them you're back in town and to come shoot you."

She rolled her eyes. "Is that why you took the long way to this house after we left Mattly's? To make sure he didn't follow us and tell anyone where we are?"

"I'm trying to protect you. Do you get that?"

She put her hand on his chest. "I know you are, and I appreciate it. But it's not fair for you to fuss at me over what happened. I didn't tell Mattly anything he hadn't already guessed. Did you really think he believed your story about us being there about a friend? I think he's smarter than that, just as he realized right off that you're an investigator. All I did was be honest to try to make him want to give us the information we needed." Her hands curled into fists and she stepped back, her eyes practically flashing sparks. "At least be honest about this. You're mad that the trip was a waste of time and you're taking it out on me."

She pushed past him, her angry strides soon echoing on the stairs. When the distant slamming of a door carried down to him, he swore and headed to the office. He only barely managed not to slam the door himself.

When he settled into his chair, his shoulders slumped with defeat. Skylar was right. Mattly wasn't dumb. He'd seen right through their cover. But that just made this situation worse. Given his partner's history with the Lancaster brothers, and Mattly's obvious suspicions about them, they might be keeping an eye on him to make sure he didn't cause them trouble. He did seem nervous even speaking about them in his own office. That alone had Trent concerned. He needed to figure out once and for all whether the brothers had anything to do with the attempts on Skylar's life, the sooner the better.

Nothing he'd learned so far pointed away from their involvement. And everything he was learning, both from Mattly and the police files he'd already read, confirmed they were likely criminals and potentially dangerous. They also had plenty of money, which meant they could afford to bribe someone to help them track Skylar electronically. They could also easily afford to give a kid like Darius Williams an expensive Heckler & Koch HK45 semi-automatic pistol and hire him to kill her, as well as others who'd tried over the years.

Right now what he needed was a copy of Martha's will. If it was the motive behind Capone's murder, it might help explain the murder attempts on Skylar. But if the only thing in it to do with her was the two hundred thousand dollars, he couldn't imagine the brothers even blinking at that amount. He'd be back at the beginning again, with the only remaining lead being the mystery about Skylar's father. The last time he'd spoken to Brice and Callum, neither had made any real headway on figuring out why he'd lived his life on the run.

He checked the time on his cell phone. The courthouse should be open for another hour or so. However, that didn't give him time to get a security guard for Skylar and still make it there to get a copy of the will before it closed. But his Hamilton County liaison for Unfinished Business probably could.

Sure enough, after a quick call the liaison said he'd head right over to the courthouse and see what he could do. While he waited, he mulled over everything he'd found out since beginning this investigation. But all he could conclude was that he didn't know much at all. Someone had made her father so nervous that he lived like a nomad and forced his family to as well. He was fearful for his daughter's safety and taught her how to survive on her own. And then, sure enough, years later she'd had to use that training to stay alive.

But why?

She'd been fine, no attempts on her life after her father's death for several years. Then, almost five years ago, she'd had to go on the run. Again, why?

The only suspects he could come up with were the Lancaster brothers. The police files pointed to them being dangerous, suspected of being deeply entrenched in organized crime. But even knowing that, it didn't seem to make sense that they'd want to kill Skylar because their mother gave her what amounted to petty cash. Maybe they weren't involved at all.

But Mattly, who apparently knew them well, obviously believed they were behind his partner's death. That alone kept them in the "persons of interest" column.

So who else was a suspect?

No one. He was drawing a complete blank.

Whoever was after Skylar was like a ghost, leaving no traces or clues behind. He'd never worked a case this frustrating before. Then again, he'd never worked a case where his emotions were clouding his judgment. He should have recused himself from the investigation the moment he and Skylar shared that first kiss.

Who was he kidding? Nothing and no one could stop him from working on this. It was *because* he cared about her that he cared so dang much about resolving the case. Which meant he needed to dig in and figure this out. And since he had no one else on his bad guy list but the Lancasters, he might as well learn more about them.

The police files went back several years, when the FBI first started looking into their business practices. There was still a huge stack of reports he hadn't gone through. While he was waiting for a copy of the will, he'd start wading through the remaining pages.

Nearly an hour passed and he hadn't discovered anything new, just report after report about people's unproven suspicions. No wonder the FBI hadn't been able to arrest them yet. Their reputation was solidly evil. But they were masters at keeping real proof of their deeds from getting into the hands of authorities. He could totally see them as the types to hire local thugs to kill their enemies, like Skylar. The fact that one of them had likely gone to Gatlinburg to then kill the thug spoke to their desperation. There had to be something about that five-year time frame that kept coming up. Then again, maybe that was a wild-goose chase. He was getting nowhere with this case.

His phone vibrated with an incoming text. He pulled it out of his pocket and was relieved to see it was from the liaison letting him know he'd emailed Trent a copy of the will. Seeing that the attachment was over sixty pages made his stomach sink. He was in for a long night.

Switching to his laptop, he opened the will document. The first thing he did was a search on the name

Skylar. There was only one hit, Skylar Montgomery, on page forty-seven. The paragraph about her spoke to the money he already knew about. And it was in the middle of several pages of similar gifts to other people, for similar amounts. She'd been generous with her friends, and what she'd given Skylar didn't stand out as unusual in any way.

So much for the quick, easy discovery he'd hoped for that would tell him why someone wanted to kill her. Now he had sixty pages of legalese to read through on the off chance that there was a golden nugget hidden in there somewhere.

An hour and about twenty dense, hard-to-read pages later, he struck gold. It might turn out to be fool's gold, but it was shiny and compelling just the same. In a section where Martha had listed members of her staff and various sentimental items she wanted them to have, there was mention of her head housekeeper. The woman was said to have faithfully worked at the Lancaster mansion for over fifty years and showed no signs of slowing down and retiring.

Her name was Abigail Flores.

Abigail. Skylar's mother was named Abigail, Abby for short. Obviously, the woman in the will was too old to be Skylar's mom. But Skylar had said her mom was named after her mother and that she'd come from Chattanooga.

The name Abigail was fairly common. There were probably hundreds of women in this city with that name. But of those, how many had a connection to the Lancaster family? Could the Abigail Flores mentioned in the will be Skylar's grandmother? And if so, what was the motive behind Abby, and now Skylar, having to go on the run?

The only thing he could think of was that the Flores family would have had access to everything in the mansion. Had the daughter, Abby, stolen something from the Lancasters? If so, what could it have been that it was worth killing her over it?

Then again, if the Lancasters were the crime family the FBI believed them to be, maybe it was all about revenge, making a statement that no one could get away with stealing from them. Maybe they'd gone after Abby first. Once they'd tracked her down years later and discovered she'd already passed away, they'd transferred their payback to Abby's child. Skylar.

Could it really be something that simple? That petty? A crime family protecting its so-called honor by killing the daughter of the woman who supposedly wronged them? It didn't seem to make sense. But in a way, it made perfect sense. That missing puzzle piece he'd talked about long ago, that little nugget of information about Skylar's mother being named after her mother, had just fallen into place. And it formed the first clear picture of this case.

When Martha Lancaster met Skylar at the hospice center, she must have noticed the resemblance to her housekeeper, Abigail. Skylar had told him that Martha often asked her questions about herself. Perhaps Skylar had revealed that her mother's name was Abby. And Martha made the connection. Trent doubted she had any ill will toward Skylar. She certainly wouldn't have bequeathed her money if she did. Maybe the theft, or whatever Abby had done, had been against the brothers and Martha didn't even know about it. In a casual conversation she could have mentioned Skylar. And they decided to finalize their revenge against the daughter of their enemy.

He sat there, thinking it through. The more he thought about it, the more he was convinced he was on to something. The actual cause of the vendetta between the brothers and Skylar's mother was an unknown. But it didn't really matter. What did matter was that there *was* a vendetta. It explained everything.

Still, it was only a hunch at this point. He was making leaps in logic based on two similarly named women. It was entirely possible that Skylar's Abby had nothing to do with the Lancasters and he was so far down the rabbit hole, he couldn't seem to find his way out.

He rubbed his eyes, then set the laptop aside to sift through the police reports. When he was trying to sort something out in his mind, he found it was sometimes better to do something else. His subconscious would noodle over it while he was focused elsewhere.

Like reading about a million pages of reports.

The FBI liked nothing more than to write reports. And what the liaison had given him was only a fraction of everything they had. It would take him days to read through everything on his desk. It had already taken days.

Shaking his head, he shoved the reports away and grabbed the stack of photographs instead. As with the files, he'd only carefully studied a handful of the pictures. He decided to thumb through them and take a better look. You never knew when another puzzle piece might fall into your lap.

Most of them were of either Richard or Scott at various functions, including horse races. He knew because he had a cross-reference—yet another report—that correlated a number on the back of each photo to a written description. A surprising number of pictures were taken in Kentucky. Then again, the family had a lot of properties there, including some impressive horse-breeding operations that eclipsed the ones here in Tennessee. It appeared from the pictures that the FBI was focused more on the activity in Kentucky. Probably made sense if they thought there was illegal gambling involved. Horse breeding begat horse racing, which begat illegal betting.

A group of pictures in the middle of the stack was more family oriented. There were all kinds of gatherings at the mansion, both inside and out. Easter egg hunts with dozens of children, probably from some charity or other. Or maybe the family's church.

One of them seemed much older than the rest. Definitely not a picture the FBI took. In this one, Martha was much younger. So was her husband, John, standing beside her with his arm around her shoulders. Her young sons stood on either side of the couple. This was obviously years before Richard married Phoebe and they had their son, Randolph. Two other people, one on each end, finished out the line. He noticed a fireplace behind the group. The person on the left seemed vaguely familiar, but Trent couldn't think of who it might be. It probably didn't matter, but he had the cross-reference handy so he looked up the picture—number 117.

When he read the names of the people, he froze. Puzzle pieces started rearranging and clicking in his mind. He grabbed the picture again and held it close. Recognition slammed into him.

No. Freaking. Way.

He grabbed his laptop and brought up the will. This time, he read every single word, all sixty ridiculously complicated and difficult-to-read pages. Hours later, he closed his laptop, stunned. He had a new theory now, one that could explain everything. But he needed proof.

And he knew just how to get it.

He needed two of the papers from the police folder that he'd skimmed earlier, but he didn't know where they were. It took some digging. Once he located them, he photographed them with his phone and sent them to the lab at Unfinished Business. Then he texted his friend Ranger McKenzie asking him to call ASAP.

His cell phone rang almost immediately. But it wasn't McKenzie. It was Brice.

"Don't get excited," Brice warned as soon as he answered. "I'm not calling with any amazing discoveries. I'm just giving you an update that I'm still coming up with a big fat zero. That's even with Callum's help—and he's been working his tail off on this. Whatever Skylar's father's real name was, he did a far better job of hiding it in the beginning when he first went on the run than he did later on. It's not that I'm giving up. Yet. But I'm dang close."

"Maybe I can help you with that," Trent said. He explained what he meant.

Brice let out a low whistle. "How sure are you about this information?"

"It's a working theory, completely circumstantial at this point. But it fits better than anything else we've come up with. I'm trying to prove it, or disprove it. Run with what I gave you and see if anything comes up."

His phone vibrated. He checked the screen. "I have another call coming in. I've got to take this."

"No problem. I'll see what I can do with this new information. Talk to you soon."

Trent pressed the accept button on his phone's screen. "McKenzie. Thanks for calling back so quickly." He explained what he wanted. McKenzie eagerly agreed to help.

"I'll call the lab at my company and have them put a rush on it," Trent told him. "They work twenty-four seven over there so it won't take long. And they have some experimental procedures to get amazingly fast results. Not proven enough to be admissible in court yet, but enough to at least give us the answers we need."

"Must be nice to have a billionaire for a boss. He makes miracles happen. Our state lab would take weeks or months to turn something like that around."

"The perks of working in the private sector."

"Now you're just rubbing it in. I'd say you owe me. But if this helps me solve the Darius Williams murder, we'll call it even. Make sure you share the lab results as soon as you get them. I'll be expecting a call. Soon."

"Will do." Trent hung up and paced back and forth across the room. The lab was fast, but in spite of McKenzie's claim about miracles, running intricate tests still took time.

His stomach rumbled. He checked the time and realized that the dinner hour had passed long ago. Had Skylar gotten something to eat? He hoped so. He also hoped she wasn't angry with him anymore. She deserved an apology. But focusing on that right now was impossible with all of these puzzle pieces floating around. He was close to the truth. He could feel it. Then again, if the answers he was seeking didn't confirm his theory, he'd be right back where he started.

No suspects. No clue how to get Skylar her life back.

An hour passed. He was too keyed-up to sit. He continued pacing and thinking. Turning the puzzle pieces different ways, trying to fit them together into another theory, just in case his suspicions were proven wrong.

His phone vibrated. Brice was calling.

"You were right," Brice said. "How did you know?"

Trent let out a relieved breath. A huge puzzle piece had just fallen into place. "Martha told me."

"Who?"

"I'll explain later. I need one more thing as final proof."

"Anything I can do?" Brice asked.

"I've got someone else working on it. I'll have the answer soon, one way or the other."

"Okay, call if you need me."

A knock sounded. When he opened the office door, an uncharacteristically uncertain-looking Skylar, now wearing a blouse and jeans, stood in the opening.

"Is it okay if I come in?" she asked.

"Of course. Always." He stood back to let her enter and followed her to the desk.

She turned around and held up a paperback book with an atmospheric cover depicting a foggy lake and an empty boat. "Today wasn't a total loss. I couldn't imagine a house this big not having at least one book somewhere, so I went on a hunt. Found this in a side table in one of the guest bedrooms. Must have been left by a previous renter. It's a fairly new release, a murder mystery I've been wanting to read. It's fascinating. I'm already a third of the way through."

"A third, huh? Impressive. That's a thick book."

"I've become a fast reader. When you spend most of your time alone without electronics to entertain you, reading is the only thing that keeps you sane. Every time I go into a town for supplies, I trade out my old books for new ones."

She set the book down and squeezed her hands together in that way he'd gotten to know so well whenever she was nervous or upset.

"About earlier," she began. "I shouldn't have—"

"Yes, you should have. You don't owe me an explanation or an apology, if you were thinking along those lines. I was a total jerk for being angry with you. What you said was true. Mattly didn't buy my pathetic cover story. It's my fault what happened today. Not yours. I'm sorry for blaming you. But even more than that, I'm sorry I took my frustration out on you. Forgive me?"

A smile bloomed on her face like a flower opening its petals to the morning sun. "You're forgiven. I'm sorry—and don't try to tell me not to say that. I really am. I shouldn't have let my temper get away with me either. I hope we can move past this and forget it."

"Forget what?" He winked, feeling much lighter of spirit even with everything else going on. It was amazing what a smile from Skylar could do to him.

"Okay, good. That's settled. I'm starving. You?"

"Actually, yes. I'd hoped you'd eaten already."

"Didn't even think about food until I came up for air

from my book. I can whip us up something light and easy, if you want, since it's getting late. Soup? An omelet? Or I could—"

"Hold that thought." His phone was buzzing with another incoming text. He read it, then read it again, slowly, carefully, to make sure he hadn't misunderstood. This was the last puzzle piece. And it fit like a dream. It explained everything.

But it also meant he had an entirely new puzzle to solve—how to keep Skylar safe going forward. Solving the mystery didn't magically make her safe as he'd hoped it would. Far from it. If anything, things were worse, much worse.

She put her hand on his arm, the corners of her eyes crinkling with concern. "Is something wrong? I mean, other than the usual?"

"Yes. No. It's complicated. Sorry, just one more minute." He made another call. "Callum, hey. If any of our investigators are still at Unfinished Business, get them into the conference room. Tag the rest of the team and have them join remotely. We need an emergency meeting. Right now. I'll head into the family room here and send a link."

"Will do. But what's the emergency?" Callum asked.

Trent met Skylar's questioning gaze as he answered. "I know who's trying to kill Skylar. And I know why they want her dead."

Chapter Nineteen

For the lateness of the hour, the family room TV showed a surprising number of investigators still at work in the company's conference room in Gatlinburg. A few others had joined the video conference from their homes, their pictures displayed in squares on the screen. Ivy was wrapped in a pink blanket in a recliner, covering her mouth as she yawned. Faith was in her home office, her hair and makeup perfect as usual. She was still wearing the suit she'd likely worn to work today.

A manila folder Trent had brought from the office was on the coffee table in front of Skylar and him on the couch. The TV displayed a dark square in the top middle where his and Skylar's picture would appear once he pressed the remote control to unmute them and turn on the camera above the TV.

He glanced at her, finger poised over the remote. "Ready to go live?"

"Can't you tell me now who wants to kill me, and why? I don't need a team meeting."

He grinned. "Don't steal my moment. I've been working my butt off trying to figure this out. If I tell you it's Colonel Mustard in the library with a candlestick without explaining how I got to that point, that'll ruin the fun."

"This isn't fun. It's nerve-wracking. I've been waiting five years to find out why my life was turned upside down."

He sobered and gently feathered her bangs back from her eyes. "I know it's hard. But this isn't something I can drop on you without putting some context around it. You wouldn't even believe me. Just as important, I could have tunnel vision since I've been working this particular angle mostly on my own. There may be something I haven't thought of that's a better explanation for what I've found out. Walking through it with the rest of the team members, who've been digging into your case too, means they may spot flaws in my conclusions. They may tell me I got it all wrong."

"I can't imagine you getting it wrong. But I see what you're saying. I'll try to be patient. I wouldn't mind following the breadcrumbs too, so I can better understand what's going on."

Unable to stop himself, he leaned in and gave her a kiss. But when he would have pulled back, she grasped the suit jacket he'd shrugged back on for the meeting and pulled him closer, moving her lips against his. He groaned and reached for her.

All the frustration, the fears about her at Mattly's earlier today, the excitement about potentially solving the case, and the sudden realization that she meant more to him than anyone had…in a very, very long time, came crashing in on him. He wanted to kiss her forever. He wanted to push her back against the cushions and love her the way he'd secretly wanted to from the moment he'd first admired her shooting skills. She was a drug that he could never get enough of. And he'd only had a very small dose. If he ever made love to her, he'd probably OD. But what a way to go.

"Trent," Callum called out. "Your audio and video aren't on yet. Is there a problem with the link? Can you see us and hear us?"

"Tell him to go away," Skylar grumbled.

He laughed and straightened her hair. "Come on, beautiful. This is what you've been waiting for."

Her face flushed with pleasure. "That's not all *I've* been waiting for." She gave him a saucy leer that had him laughing again.

"Trent?" Callum called out. "Maybe we should rejoin the link. Something's wrong."

"Go ahead." Skylar tugged her shirt and cleared her throat.

He clicked the remote and the dark square on the TV was replaced with a picture of him and Skylar sitting beside each other on the couch. "Can you see us now? Do you hear us?"

"There they are." Callum gave him a thumbs-up. "You're getting just as bad with electronics as I am."

Trent chuckled at his friend's mistaken belief that the delay was caused by a glitch. "It'll take a lot more than one problem to put me on your level of electronic ineptitude."

Callum laughed. "The gang's all here, minus Grayson, Willow and Ryland, of course. Still on their respective vacations."

Ivy tapped her computer camera. "Let's get this meeting going. I need my beauty sleep."

"No, you don't," Skylar assured her. "You're always gorgeous."

Ivy flashed her a big smile. "I knew I liked you."

Everyone quieted down as Trent launched into his explanation of why he'd been focusing on the Lancaster brother angle for the attempts on Skylar's life. He reminded them about the day at the hospice center, after he'd discovered the shooter could have walked through the woods from the Lancaster home to where Martha was staying at the center. He pointed out that the brothers were suspected of being in organized crime and the FBI was investigating them. The fact that Skylar's troubles had started after Martha's death and that the first shooter could have come from the Lancaster property seemed too coincidental for his liking. He'd been looking for a way to prove, or disprove, a link ever since.

After discovering that the lawyer who'd worked on Martha's will had been murdered shortly after her death, and that he'd actually met earlier with Skylar at the hospice center, he decided to delve into that angle too. He brought them up to speed about their visit with the dead lawyer's partner. He explained that Mattly believed Richard and Scott Lancaster had killed his partner over Martha's will.

"Did you get a copy of the will?" someone asked.

"I did, earlier today from our Chattanooga PD liaison. It's dense reading, a ton of legal language to wade through. My first pass I found where Martha had bequeathed two hundred thousand dollars to Skylar Montgomery."

"Hardly a motive for murder," Callum said. "The Lancaster estate is worth a ton more than that."

"Plus, dozens of other beneficiaries are listed in the will with similar monetary amounts," Trent said. "That proved to me that the money Martha gave to Skylar wasn't substantial to her estate. It didn't raise any red flags."

"So you're keeping us up late to tell us you've basically got nothing?" Callum complained.

Brice frowned at the camera. "When did you get so grumpy, *old man*? Let Trent talk. He's got a lot more than nothing. You'll see."

"Hold it." Callum straightened. "Brice, you've got an inside scoop you didn't share with me? We've both been working together on this."

"Didn't have time."

"Children," Ivy called out. "Be quiet and let Trent get on with this."

"Herding cats," Skylar whispered.

Trent smiled. "Skylar's name wasn't the only one I saw in Martha's will that gave me pause. There was one in the section where she bequeathed money to members of her staff. She gave a generous sum to her head housekeeper who's been working in the mansion for over fifty years." He glanced at Skylar as he continued. "Her name is Abigail Flores."

The name didn't register with her. She showed no reaction.

"Something you all don't know," he continued, "is that Skylar's mother was named Abigail too, Abby for short. And Skylar believes she came from Chattanooga."

That got Skylar's attention.

She frowned. "What are you saying? My mom died years ago. And even if she hadn't, it's not like she'd hide out at the Lancaster mansion. Besides, this Abigail Flores is old enough to be my grandmother." Her eyes widened.

"You're right. Didn't you tell me once that your mother was named after her mother? Both of them were Abigail."

"Hold it, hold it." This time it was Ivy who interrupted. "Trent, you're really reaching. So there's a woman working for the Lancasters named Abigail. How does that shed light on anything? I don't see how this matters one way or the other. Do you have proof she's related to Skylar, DNA?"

"No hard proof. No DNA. But I strongly believe that Abigail Flores is Skylar's grandmother. Why I believe that will become clear soon, and it goes to motive." He glanced at Skylar. "How are you holding up? Are you okay?"

She slowly nodded. "I'm with Ivy on this, unconvinced. Confused, but fine."

"All right. I'm going to hold a picture up toward the camera. You all might have to zoom in on the screen to get a good look at it. This is one from the FBI's investigation into the Lancaster brothers. It's a recent surveillance photo of some staff members coming to the mansion to start work. The woman in the middle with dark eyes and dark hair, that's Flores." He held it up for the others and it displayed on the TV.

"May I see that?" Skylar held out her hand.

He gave her the picture. She held it close, her eyes widening. "Honestly, she does favor how I remember my mom. A lot. Same hair and eyes. Same nose, mouth. Do you really think she's my grandmother?"

It was funny how people often didn't see the similarities between someone else and themselves. When he'd first seen a picture of the housekeeper, he'd seen Skylar.

"I do."

She swallowed and continued to stare at the picture.

"At the risk of sounding like Callum," Ivy said, "Relevance? You said it goes to motive."

He told them his first theory about Flores, that maybe her daughter—Abby—had stolen something or maybe even saw something she shouldn't have and went on the run.

"But when I found this picture, it sent me down another path entirely." He pulled out the second photo he'd brought to the family room and held it up toward the camera.

Skylar was still looking at the picture of Abigail Flores.

"This new photo is from decades ago, showing the Lancasters posing in front of a fireplace, presumably at the mansion here in Chattanooga. Not an FBI surveillance photo, obviously. I'm not sure how they got hold of this one. It appears to be an old family picture."

Callum leaned close to his monitor. "Not exclusively. There are six people. I see Martha, her deceased husband, John, their two sons—Richard and Scott. I'm guessing the woman on the right is part of the staff since she's wearing an apron. Who's the guy on the far left? I doubt he's the hired help, not in that expensive-looking suit."

"That would be Brandon Lancaster. Martha's oldest son."

"Wait," Ivy said. "There's another son?"

Skylar glanced up at the TV. Trent knew the moment recognition hit. Her face went pale.

He took her hand in his. "There was a third son, the oldest son. He disappeared years ago after having a falling out with the family and was never seen again. One of the names he was known by over the years after he left was Ryan Montgomery. Skylar's father."

There was a collective gasp from the other investigators.

Skylar started slowly shaking her head, her gaze riveted to the screen. "No. It can't be. It doesn't... I don't believe it." The look on her face told him that part of her did. But she didn't *want* to believe it.

He threaded his fingers through hers. "I have proof for this part of my theory. Brice used his military intelligence contact to confirm that Brandon Lancaster was an Army Ranger stationed in Germany for the time frame we were interested in. His commanding officer verified that Brandon had family troubles, that he had two brothers named Richard and Scott. He also confirmed that Brandon married a young woman while there, a woman he'd flown into Germany from Tennessee shortly after he arrived. Her name was Abigail Flores. Everyone called her Abby."

Her hand tightened on his. "You're saying my mother was the daughter of the head housekeeper?"

"Yes. I believe she and the eldest son were in love and the family disapproved. He joined the military to make it on his own, then sent back for Abby. Later, when his family tried to find him, he quit the military as soon as his contract was up, changed their names and started moving on a regular basis so his family wouldn't find them."

She shook her head. "Even if that's true." She cleared her throat, looking mildly stunned. "Even if you're right, that can't possibly be a motive for them wanting to kill me all these years later, could it? Because they hate that I exist, as proof that their son, their brother, what, married beneath them?" She tugged her hand free. "You're wrong." She glanced up at the screen, then looked away. "You have to be wrong."

"Skylar, I have DNA."

"DNA? From my dad? How?"

"Not your dad. You. You gave Ranger McKenzie a DNA sample for his investigation into the death of the Gatlinburg shooter. The FBI gathered DNA samples from Richard and Scott from discarded fast-food drink cups long ago without them knowing. I had McKenzie send your sample to our lab because his lab was too backed up to even take it yet. Our lab has an experimental procedure that provides DNA preliminary results really quickly. Plus, there were two reports in the Chattanooga police folder I got, DNA profiles the FBI had already done on the brothers to use for comparison. The lab texted me earlier tonight. Richard and Scott Lancaster are conclusively your uncles. By default, Brandon Lancaster was your father."

Probably without even realizing she was doing it, she pressed her hand against the compass necklace that her father had given her. The outline of the compass was barely visible through her shirt.

He desperately wanted to hold her, regardless of how it might look to his fellow investigators. She seemed so lost and confused. But she'd scooted farther away from him and he doubted she'd let him touch her right now if he tried.

"Trent," Callum called out. "These are startling revelations. But I'm still not sure I follow why it's a motive for murder."

"Remember when I mentioned the will was full of legalese and sixty pages long? It took me a while to get through the whole thing. I stopped and started several times in between calls. When I finally read the whole thing, the motive was right there in black and white, like someone hitting me over the head with a hammer."

"Inheritance," Ivy offered. "The brothers are worried that Skylar could claim her father's share if she takes them to court."

Skylar looked up at the TV, her brows furrowed. "Why would they worry about me trying to get their money? I didn't even know I was related to them." She shivered and rubbed her hands up and down her arms. "Just knowing their blood runs through my veins makes me sick."

"It's your father's blood too," Trent reminded her. "And he was a good man. Brice said your dad spoke to his commanding officer about his home life. They were close friends. Your father didn't approve of the family's criminal side of their business ventures. And his family didn't approve of Abby. Brandon left to get away from them and pursue a life on his own terms, with the woman he loved. He cut the family off, not the other way around."

She clutched the compass again through her shirt but didn't say anything.

"So that's it?" Callum asked. "The oldest son disowned the family and went into hiding to avoid them. And then the younger sons somehow discovered that Skylar existed—"

"From Martha," Trent said. "I believe Martha recognized that Skylar looked like her son, and the housekeeper, and believed she might be her granddaughter. She and Skylar spoke about her past. I imagine Martha got enough information to feel certain that Skylar was the daughter of Brandon and Abby. Martha loved Brandon very much, seemed to have favored him over her other sons. I believe she tried to find him over the years and came close a few times. That's why Skylar's dad kept moving the family around. As for trying to kill you, Skylar, I believe that's all on the younger brothers. The FBI reports paint the picture of sons who didn't get along with their mother. Her will backs that up and provides the motive."

Skylar wrapped her arms around her waist. "If you're going to say she left me everything, that doesn't make sense. You said my name was only listed once, when she bequeathed two hundred thousand dollars to me."

"True. Your name wasn't mentioned anywhere else, not explicitly. But once I finally read to the end of the will, I found the Brandon Lancaster name. And that of course led me to discover he was your father. Martha Lancaster left generous annual stipends for Richard and Scott, and they reap the benefits of the family's businesses, for now. But Martha left the bulk of her liquid assets—hundreds of millions of dollars—and ownership of the family businesses in an unbreakable trust that Albert Capone set up for her. All of those assets, far more than Richard and Scott received, is held for her son if he's found alive. If not, then the estate passes to any children he had, again, if proven. And if there are no children, everything reverts to the brothers."

Brice let out a low whistle. "That's a heck of a motive for murder."

"It gets worse," Trent said. "There's a deadline, extra incentive for them to find her now. The clause giving the estate to Skylar expires exactly five years after Martha's death, which is in just a few days. The brothers have hundreds of millions of reasons why they need to find her and prevent her from claiming their fortune. They've known about her for years and have tried numerous times to eliminate her. They have no way of knowing whether or not she knows she's a Lancaster, and whether she's planning on dropping in right before the deadline to claim her inheritance. By now they have to be getting desperate to make sure that doesn't happen. Because of that five-year deadline coming up soon, they probably have an army of people hunting for her everywhere they've ever gotten a lead about her including Gatlinburg. Their goal is to find her in the next forty-eight hours and kill her."

Skylar wrung her hands together. "What do we do? We should leave, right? Go someplace I've never been before."

Trent and everyone on the screen shook their heads *no.*

Ivy volunteered the information before anyone else spoke up. "Your alleged grandmother lives here. You used to live here. If you know about the will and want the money, it would make sense you'd lie low in Chattanooga until you can safely contact the trustees of the will. You can bet the brothers are watching the trustees and have people all over town on the alert for any sightings of you. With incentive like that, they're watching the highways in and out of Chattanooga in particular, checking rest stops, gas and food exits. They can afford it, and they won't scrimp. They want you found."

"I agree," another investigator volunteered. "Being on the road is more dangerous at this point than staying put. As long as no one can make the connections and figure out where you're staying, you're safer where you are. Unless you did something to connect your Montgomery identity to the alias that was used at the hospice facility. What about the lawyer you talked to? Mattly?"

Skylar started shaking again. "I screwed up. I flat-out told him I knew Martha, that she'd left me money in the will."

"No, I screwed up," Trent said. "I shouldn't have let you go there in the first place. But Mattly seems like a decent guy. And he hates the Lancaster brothers. I don't think he'd say anything."

"Uh, guys?" Brice looked up from his phone. "I just did a quick search on that Mattly fellow. He's all over the Chattanooga news. He was found murdered in his law office about an hour ago."

Skylar sucked in a sharp breath. "Oh, no. Poor Mr. Mattly. You don't think the Lancaster brothers found him, do you?"

Trent jumped to his feet. "I think that's exactly what happened. They probably tortured him, confirmed you're here in town. By now, their contacts are looking into recent rentals to a couple that meets our description. The meeting's over. We're leaving. Now."

He grabbed Skylar's hand.

"Wait. My purse, our things—"

"We'll send someone back for them later. I'll call 911, tell the police to meet us a few miles away from here." He motioned toward the TV while still looking at her. "The team will follow protocol for when one of us is in danger. They'll hit the road, head straight here. We'll call them again once we're away from the house and I can map out an escape route. Is that clear everyone?" He looked up at the TV. The screen was dark. Had the connection been lost? There wasn't time to worry about it. "Come on."

He pulled out his cell phone and punched 911 as they crossed the room toward the door to the garage. He suddenly stopped and looked at his phone. Frowning, he pressed the buttons again, then held it to his ear.

"What's wrong?" she asked.

"Signal's not going through."

"Have you had a problem like that before in this house?"

"No. It's almost like the signals being jam—" He jerked his head up and looked through the dining room archway toward the front windows. "Skylar! Get down!"

He threw himself on top of her as automatic gunfire ripped through the walls.

Chapter Twenty

The gunfire stopped. Shouts sounded from outside.

"Can't breathe." Skylar pushed at Trent to get off her.

He rolled to the side, his brow furrowed with concern. "Are you hit?"

"No. But I was almost crushed to death by a six foot two fashion model masquerading as an investigator."

He laughed. "People are trying to kill us and you have me laughing. Unbelievable."

"It's a gift. We need to get to your SUV."

"Agreed. Ten feet to the garage door. I vote we crawl. Hopefully they won't see us through any of the windows."

A loud bang sounded on the front door. "They won't be outside much longer."

"Go, go." He pushed her ahead of him.

Skylar reached up and opened the door between the house and the garage, then scurried inside. Trent scrambled in after her and quietly clicked the door shut. Then he jumped up and lowered a metal bar across it.

She motioned toward the bar as she stood. "That's not standard equipment in a rental."

"I had it installed before we got here. Always be prepared. That's my motto."

"You were a Boy Scout?"

"Heck no."

She rolled her eyes.

More gunshots sounded from outside, but thankfully none of them came through the garage walls.

She winced. "See, I told you gunfights are never planned."

"Yes, you did. But unplanned and unprepared are two different things."

"You're sure you weren't a Scout?"

"Well, I tried. They kicked me out. My methods were too dangerous for their tastes."

"Shocking."

"You're enjoying this far too much," he chided.

"I'd rather go down fighting than cower in fear."

"No one's going down. These jerks picked the wrong people to mess with." He rounded the front of the SUV to the driver's side.

"Please tell me you have the keys." She jumped into the front passenger seat.

He opened the door behind the driver's seat. "They're in the console. But we're not taking the SUV. They'll expect that. It'll be a death trap." He grabbed a black backpack from the floorboard and unzipped it.

"Holy smokes," she said. "You have an arsenal in there."

"We'll need it." Another loud bang sounded from inside, making him wince. "Sounds like they just destroyed the front door. They're in the house now."

She grabbed the keys and unlocked the glove box. Her gun was still inside from when they'd met with

Mattly. “There you are, baby.” She checked the loading. For once Trent hadn’t taken out the magazine.

More loud noises sounded from inside.

“They’re searching for us,” she said, lowering her voice. “What’s the plan?”

“Kevlar first.” He yanked a vest out, then leaned over the back seat and grabbed another one that he pitched to her. “Put that on. Hurry.”

As they both shrugged into their vests, she marveled at the perfect fit of hers. “You had a vest specifically for me, didn’t you?”

“Just in case. I sure had hoped not to need it, though.” He motioned toward the front left side of the garage. “Valet door. That’s our exit. But they’ll be watching, guaranteed. No matter where we go, we’re going to have to run a gauntlet to make it to tree cover.”

“There’s only fifteen feet of open ground outside that door before we’ll reach the woods. If we lay enough cover fire, we can do it.”

He arched a brow. “How do you know it’s fifteen feet?”

“I scoped out our surroundings from an upstairs window when we first arrived. Always know where your exits are.”

“That didn’t work so well for you back in the Smoky Mountains National Park. I seem to recall you getting cornered.”

“One mistake. One mistake in five years and he throws it in my face.”

He shook his head, grinning. “All right. Let’s do this. I’ll fire left, you fire right when we head out that valet door. But first, we need a diversion to give us a fighting chance. Duck down between the front of the SUV and the wall. The engine block should shield you from any bullets when I open the garage door."

"Wait. You're going to open the door? The big one that's hiding where we are?"

"No time to explain. Hurry."

She swore and got out of the truck, then hunkered down on the concrete step-up behind the engine block, her back to the wall.

A crashing noise sounded from inside the house. It was far too close. "Hurry," she whispered. "Whatever you're going to do, make it fast."

"Working on it."

She couldn't tell what he was doing from her vantage point, but seconds later the engine started. Almost immediately, someone rattled the knob on the door between the family room and the garage. She trained her pistol on it and sent up a silent prayer that Trent could create whatever diversion he had in mind before the bad guys busted inside.

The exterior garage door started sliding up in a painfully slow crawl.

More yelling came from outside. A bullet shot through the opening. Skylar ducked behind the tire, aiming her pistol up toward the ceiling, afraid to shoot without knowing where Trent was.

Suddenly the truck's tires shrieked. It tore off, backing out of the garage and barreling down the driveway. Men dived to the side to get out of the way.

"Now," Trent yelled.

She took off running. He threw the valet door open and they both sprinted outside, laying down cover fire as they ran. Moments later, they ducked behind two large oak trees and glanced at each other.

"I can't believe we made it," she said.

"Me either."

She laughed. "What's part two of your plan?"

"Run like hell."

They both looked back toward the house. Three men were running up the driveway toward them. Two more came from the rear yard and another rounded the corner from the front of the house.

"I count six bad guys," she said.

"Let's even up the numbers a bit."

They both leaned around the trees and started firing. A guttural scream sounded as one of the men fell to the ground. Another scream.

"I got two," she bragged.

"One of those was mine."

Automatic gunfire strafed at them from off to their left through the trees.

"Another bad guy," she yelled.

"With a more powerful weapon than we have. Run!"

They took off again, zigzagging and shooting over their shoulders whenever they caught a break in the trees.

A few minutes later, Trent called a halt and they both crouched down back-to-back with their pistols out, gasping for breath. He dropped his backpack beside them, grabbed two magazines and handed them to her.

"Reload," he whispered.

"Bless you. I was almost out."

"Me too."

They both shoved magazines into their guns and

pocketed a spare. He zipped up the backpack and hurriedly put it on.

The gunshots stopped. The sudden silence was unnerving.

"They must be close," she whispered. "They're hunting us."

"We need to take advantage of the terrain. I should have gone online and gotten a satellite view of the area days ago."

"Lucky for you, I already did that too. It's all part of that *know your exits* thing."

"Bless you." He grinned. "Where to?"

She jerked her head. "West, young man. Go west."

"You've been reading too many books."

She looked shocked. "You can never read too many books. Like I said, west."

"That's where the automatic gunfire was coming from earlier," he reminded her.

"I know. But everyone else is on our tail, catching up. Like you said, we have to use the terrain. There's a canyon and a waterfall not much farther. If we can make it there, we might have a chance."

"I have another idea. Backup." He pulled out his cell phone, then swore. "Whoever was jamming the signal earlier isn't jamming it anymore. But I don't have any bars. No reception out here. All right. Let's go, as quickly and quietly as possible. Stay low."

She nodded and they both headed through the woods again, with her leading the way. She knew from his swearing when she started out that he didn't want her in front. He wanted to protect her, use his body as a shield in case the shooter with the automatic weapon found them. But she was the only one who knew where the canyon was. It made sense for her to take the lead.

A few moments later, a loud thump sounded behind her. She whirled around to see Trent wiping a bloody blade on the chest of a dead gunman at his feet. She hadn't even realized he had a knife, much less one that large and lethal-looking. And then it dawned on her just how close the gunman had gotten to her. Good grief, she'd never even heard him. Trent had saved her life.

He pulled up the leg of his dress pants and shoved the knife in his boot. The incongruity of him in a suit, running through the woods, with a foot-long knife shoved in his boot and a backpack of ammunition suddenly had her wanting to laugh. But it wasn't funny. It was terrifying. The odds were against them no matter how good they both might be at surviving. They were going to die.

She started to shake so hard she nearly dropped her pistol.

He pulled her behind a large tree, then kissed her. When he pulled back, he searched her gaze. "Better?"

She choked on a laugh. "Apparently. I'm no longer shaking or near hysterics."

He smiled and ran a finger down the column of her throat as if they had all the time in the world. "We're going to make it, Skylar. Trust me."

The bone-chilling fear that had sunk its talons in her moments earlier suddenly lifted. She did trust him. And she trusted herself. They could do this. They had to do this. Because she refused to die in the stupid woods at the hands of thugs her own uncles had hired to kill her. She wanted justice. And to get that, she had to fight.

She straightened and checked her magazine before popping it back in her pistol. "Ready. Let's go."

He nodded approvingly and they took off again.

The men chasing them weren't doing a good job of being quiet. Perhaps they sensed how close they were to their prey and didn't feel the need for stealth. Panic started eroding Skylar's confidence again. A laugh sounded somewhere not far behind. She faltered, but Trent's firm hand grasped her arm and kept her from falling.

Another sound whispered through the trees up ahead.

She looked at Trent. "Water," she whispered.

He nodded and they put on a burst of speed.

Picturing the online satellite images in her mind, she tried to orient herself as to where they were. She yanked out the compass hanging around her neck and checked the direction, thought back on when they'd come into the woods, the turns they'd made. Everything clicked together in her mind like a perfect map. They should be almost to the—

"Stop!" She threw herself at Trent, knocking him sideways against a tree. They both fell to the ground and rolled a few more feet, stopping at the very edge of the cliff.

Trent swore and yanked her back, pulling her with him until they were out of danger.

"Good grief, that was close," he whispered against her hair.

Thrashing sounded from the woods.

"This is our chance," she whispered back. She pointed at some downed branches near the cliff's edge. "We have to conceal it."

He jumped up and grabbed the branches. Together they pulled them just far enough so it wasn't obvious that the very next step was into open air with a fifty-foot drop to the rocky stream below.

Thumping sounds indicated the gunmen would be upon them any moment.

She quickly whispered what she wanted Trent to do.

He vigorously shook his head no and whispered that it was too dangerous.

A shout sounded. A bullet whistled past her ear.

Trent fired back, dropping the man like a rock. But she heard more coming. They sounded like a herd of horses thundering toward her and Trent.

And the cliff.

"Okay," he silently mouthed, perhaps realizing they had no other viable option. He'd do it her way.

He whipped his belt out of his pant loops and wrapped it around a branch on an oak tree and then around his wrist. Stepping just behind the concealment of the branches he'd placed near the edge of the cliff, he leaned out toward her, his face lined with worry.

Five gunmen emerged from the trees, running full-on toward her. From their grins and catcalls, they thought they had her. One of them raised his gun.

"Now," she yelled.

She lunged behind the branches toward Trent.

He grabbed her around the waist, using the belt to swing them both around the tree's trunk and back to solid ground. He pulled her on top of him as he fell back, nearly crushing her with an iron grip.

Shots rang out as their pursuers galloped toward the opening in the branches where she'd disappeared. At the last moment, they must have realized their mistake. One of them screamed and tumbled over the cliff. The others slid and grabbed at each other, desperately trying to stop their momentum. Instead, like a pack of lemmings, they all plunged over the edge, their terrified screams carrying back to Skylar and Trent. Then, blissful silence.

They lay there, struggling for breath as they held onto each other.

Finally, Trent scooted backward, pulling her with him once again until they were a good six feet from the edge.

"You okay?" he asked.

"I can't believe it. But, yes."

His gaze fell to her arm and he frowned. "You're bleeding. Badly."

She looked down. "Dang. Must have cut it on one of the branches."

He threw his backpack down and ripped off his Kevlar. Buttons popped and flew as he tore off his dress shirt and wrapped it around her forearm.

She cried out when he pulled it tight.

"Sorry, sweetheart. I have to stop the bleeding."

His endearment went a long way toward easing her pain. "I know, I know."

"I'll kiss it and make it better. Later." He winked.

She laughed. "Look who else has the gift of making someone laugh in ridiculous circumstances."

"I learned from the best. Can you stand?"

"My arm's hurt, not my legs. Of course I can— Look out!"

A gunman lunged through the trees at them, aiming his rifle directly at Trent.

Skylar rolled and kicked his knee. Trent whirled around and slugged him in the throat. The man dropped to the ground, gurgling and wheezing as he grabbed for his throat and his knee at the same time, writhing in pain.

It was Scott Lancaster.

Trent kicked the weapon out of Lancaster's reach and lifted Skylar up and over him. He set her down well away from Scott, then handed her Scott's automatic weapon.

"I'll tie him up." He pulled some nylon cord out of the backpack and got on his knees behind the gasping man.

She smiled. Of course her hero had a rope in his backpack. Why wouldn't he? She checked the loading on Lancaster's gun, admiring the beauty of it. "This is some amazing hardware."

"Too bad it's wasted on this silver-spoon idiot. He should have been able to kill us ten times over and never came close. Now we know why he and his sibling hired others to do their killings."

He halted in the process of tying Scott and stared at Skylar. "Where's his brother?"

They both jerked their heads toward the trail. A dark shadow sprinted toward them. Trent and Skylar dove to the side and rolled into the cover of trees as gunshots rang out and Richard let out a guttural yell. He must have seen his brother on the ground and come running.

They both leveled their weapons toward the opening where he'd have to pass to reach the clearing.

Seconds later, Richard appeared, swinging his gun toward Skylar.

She pulled the trigger. The beautiful automatic rifle jammed.

Richard was suddenly jerked off his feet by Trent and slammed against a tree. A sickening crack sounded and blood darkened the bark. His eyes rolled up in his head as he slid to the ground, dead.

Trent stepped over him without even glancing down. He ignored the gasping, wheezing Scott and barely slowed to scoop Skylar up in his arms. She clung to him, shaking uncontrollably. Too much. It was just too much.

"Shh," he whispered. "Hear that? Sirens heading this way. Somebody must have heard the gunfire and called the police. Or maybe my team did when they couldn't reach me. We're going to be okay. We'll get that arm patched up in no time."

She nodded and tightened her good arm around his neck. "We'll go a lot faster if you let me walk."

"No."

"Trent. I'm serious. Please. I want out of these woods. Now. Put me down."

He grumbled and set her to her feet. "You sure? I'm fine carrying you."

"And I'm fine walking. I'll bet I can even run." She took off jogging toward the house to prove it.

"Skylar, look out for the—"

She slammed her shin into a fallen log and tumbled over it. Her head smacked against a tree and everything went dark.

"SIR, SIR, YOU need to put her down so we can help her."

Trent reluctantly laid his precious burden on the ambulance gurney. "She hit her head really hard. And her arm—"

"We see it, sir. We've got this." The EMTs went to work on Skylar right there in the driveway of the rental house, checking her vital signs.

Trent gave a quick briefing to the police who were already swarming the property. He told them about Scott and Richard Lancaster and where to find them.

The policeman in charge of the scene shouted orders to his men, who took off through the woods. "There's room in the ambulance for two," he told the EMTs as they loaded Skylar into the back. "If she's stable, hold for a moment so we can get the wounded guy in there too."

"To hell with that," Trent growled. "Get him a different ambulance. There's no room for him here." He hauled himself up into the back and sat on the second gurney, daring the policeman to tell him no.

The EMTs took their cue from Trent. One of them hopped up in the back and closed the doors. The other jumped into the driver's seat. Soon they were speeding down the driveway on the way to the hospital, without the affront of having Scott Lancaster in the same vehicle as Skylar.

Chapter Twenty-One

Trent set his coffee cup on the hospital room's bedside table and held Skylar's hand again. She seemed bewildered this morning with so many of Unfinished Business's investigators crowded into her room. Even the boss and his wife were there, and the lead investigator, Ryland, having cut their vacations short as soon as they'd heard about the attack on Trent and Skylar.

It was Grayson, in his thousand-dollar business suit, who'd smoothed things over with the hospital administrator to allow all of them up here at one time. Trent doubted that Erlanger East Hospital had ever had this many visitors in one room before.

But that's how his team rolled. They were as tight-knit as any family. And even though Trent wasn't hurt, just knowing he could have been killed had them driving through the night or, in some cases, flying to check on him. He was exceedingly grateful that Callum had stopped at the house and convinced a cop to let him get Trent some clean clothes even though they'd still been processing the home as a crime scene. The fresh suit that Callum had grabbed wasn't as comfortable as jeans would have been, but it beat the hospital scrubs he'd been given in the ER when he'd arrived in the ambulance half-naked.

He wasn't sure if his team's support was because this was his "pet project" case or whether they'd guessed just how much Skylar meant to him. Maybe both. He certainly wasn't hiding that he cared about her. He'd only let go of her hand to eat breakfast and drink his coffee since the team had arrived.

"Overwhelming seeing them all at once, in person, huh?" he teased her.

"It's just…crazy different being around this many people. I'm used to being by myself." Her cheeks flushed. "And I'm embarrassed that I can't remember all of your names from the video calls we had. I'm so sorry."

"Don't be. It's far easier for us to learn one name than for you to learn all of ours. I'll point everyone out. And there won't be a test afterward. There are a couple dozen support staffers in Gatlinburg, mostly lab rats and computer nerds. But this is most of the core team. There are eleven of us, counting the boss." He motioned toward the foot of the bed. "Meet Grayson Prescott, our founder and benefactor. The lovely lady beside him is his wife, Willow, who's also our victim's advocate."

They smiled and told her they were happy to meet her as Trent continued pointing out the others. "Lance Cabrera, Faith Lancaster—no relation to the Chattanooga Lancasters—Asher Whitfield, Brice Galloway, Ivy Shaw. Our liaison with the Tennessee Bureau of Investigation isn't here yet. Her name's Rowan Knight. The guy on the far right by the window is Ryland Beck, lead investigator. That's the team."

"Hey, hey," Callum called out. "You forgot me."

"No he didn't," Ryland teased. "He was *trying* to forget you."

"Yeah, yeah. I'm just glad *you're* back so I'm off the hook now as acting lead."

"You may not be glad once I return to the office," Ryland quipped. "I hear there are some expense reports we need to talk about."

Callum shrugged. "I'm going to borrow one of Trent's mottos. 'It's easier to ask for forgiveness—'"

"'—than to get permission'," everyone said.

Skylar laughed. "Seriously? That's one of your mottos?"

"I might have said it a time or two."

Everyone laughed this time.

Skylar addressed the team. "I'll try to remember your names going forward. I'm in awe that you dropped everything to come here. Especially when there really isn't anything wrong with me." She raised her right arm covered in a white bandage from elbow to wrist. "Being admitted to the hospital for what amounts to a scratch is ridiculous."

"Twenty stitches isn't a scratch," Trent said. "And they admitted you because of that nasty bump on your head. You lost consciousness. The neurologist wants to keep you overnight for observation."

She gave him a disgruntled look at the reminder about her clumsiness in falling over a log.

"Since you're all here," he said, "we might as well address the elephant in the room. Richard Lancaster is no longer a threat. But his brother, Scott, is. And who's to say that Richard's widow, Phoebe, won't step in on her husband's and teenaged son's behalf and still try to meet that deadline to keep Skylar from inheriting? The Lancasters still have millions of incentives to want her dead. They're very much a threat. And now they know where she is, courtesy of the media who got wind of the shootout."

Skylar tensed. He rubbed his thumb across the back of her hand, letting her know without words that he was there for her. But this needed to be addressed. They still had to figure out how to protect her, long-term.

"We stop the clock," Callum suggested. "We let the will's trustees know that Skylar is the legal heir. I'm sure the court will order new DNA tests. It will be a long process. But at least the financial incentive to kill her will be gone. Even better, she can have her own will drawn up declaring non-Lancaster beneficiaries, making doubly sure there's no reason for them to go after her."

Trent shook his head. "While I agree she should get her inheritance, that won't solve the problem of how to keep her safe. Revenge is a powerful motivator. I can't see the Lancasters letting Richard's death go without some kind of retribution. They'll still blame Skylar."

She tugged his hand, drawing his attention. "They'll blame you too. Richard may have started the gunfight. But you finished it. You're in danger as much as I am."

"Probably so. The local police can pursue an attempted murder charge against Scott. But he'll likely drag it out for years before doing prison time—if he even goes to prison. No telling what kinds of legal stunts he'll pull. I can name a handful of uber-wealthy murderers who paid so-called experts to confuse juries. How do you fight a crooked multimillionaire like Richard Lancaster and expect to win?"

Grayson crossed his arms. "You give him what he values most. Money. Skylar, how do you feel about giving up some of the fortune that your grandmother left in trust for you to buy off the Lancasters?"

Trent shook his head. "No way. It's her money and wrong on so many levels for a victim to pay off the perpetrator."

"I'm not a victim. I'm a survivor, always have been. If my continued survival means giving them money I never expected to get anyway, I'm all for it. It's worth it to buy myself a life. Grayson, how do we go about this?"

He gave Trent an apologetic glance before answering. "I've brokered hundreds of business deals over the years. I can make the offer, have a contract drawn up. We'll agree to increase their annual stipend every year that Skylar is safe. The increases will have to be significant to ensure that their greed outweighs their desire for revenge."

"I don't like it," Trent said. "The plan isn't fail-proof. They could always change their minds and decide their vendetta is more important than the next stipend increase."

"Nothing's fail-proof except putting them in prison," Grayson said. "But the FBI's been investigating for years. None of the recent events provides evidence to support federal charges. This proposed contract could be a stopgap until the FBI comes through, if they ever do. I could add an annual renewal option so Skylar can reevaluate and change her mind."

She pulled her hand free from Trent's and twisted

both of her hands together. "I'm trying to envision my future life. Even with this agreement, I'd need bodyguards, security at my home, wherever that might be. I'd have to constantly look over my shoulder like I've been doing for years. I got a taste of a normal life this past week and I liked it. I'm not interested in hiding away and becoming a hermit again."

Grayson nodded. "I completely understand. But if we don't get enough prosecutable evidence to put Scott, and maybe even Richard's wife, Phoebe, away for good, we don't have many options. Unless someone else has a suggestion?"

A knock sounded on the door and a nurse walked in. Her eyes widened when she saw how many people were crowded inside.

"I'm sorry but you all need to leave to give the patient privacy while I check her vitals and prep her for the doctor's visit. He'll be here in a few minutes. The waiting room is down the hall, to your left."

Grayson stepped forward and introduced himself. Trent grinned at how flustered she became with the attention of such a polished and obviously well-off businessman in his power suit.

"Is there a private room, perhaps a conference room, where my team can meet? We won't take long. We need to brainstorm some ideas. Or should I speak to Mrs. Wilkerson again, the hospital administrator? She was very understanding of our situation when I spoke to her earlier."

She swallowed nervously. "There might be a doctor consultation room available. It would be tight and there aren't enough chairs for everyone. But you could probably all fit."

"That sounds perfect. Thank you."

She nodded, looking relieved that he'd accepted her suggestion rather than argue. She explained where the room was and everyone headed out, except Trent.

"Nurse, could I have a moment with the patient before I leave?"

"Um, okay. But only a minute. I need to finish before the doctor arrives."

"Thank you."

After the nurse was gone, he took Skylar's hand again.

"You have me wondering if you have a hand fetish as much as you keep holding mine."

"It's more serious than that. I have a Skylar fetish. An obsession, really."

Her eyes widened. "That sounds serious."

"It is. I wanted to tell you that I—" His phone buzzed in his pocket. He sighed and pulled it out to check the screen. It was the FBI agent he'd been talking to off and on since the shootout, the one working on the Lancaster case. He texted a quick reply and shoved the phone back in his pocket. "I'm sorry, Skylar." Him telling her he cared about her was going to have to wait a little longer. "I have to go."

"I understand. Your team is waiting for you."

He was going to correct her assumption that it was his team he needed to see, but a knock on the door announced the nurse's return. This time she was pushing a rolling computer cart. As soon as she saw him, she frowned.

"I'm going, I'm going." He kissed Skylar's cheek. "Be good. Don't argue with the doctor."

"As long as he promises to let me out of here in the morning, I won't."

He laughed at the nurse's stern look and hurried out. When he entered the family waiting room, the FBI agent who'd texted him waved from the far left corner. Trent nodded and started toward him, then stopped when another familiar-looking face caught his attention.

An older, dark-eyed woman with gray-streaked dark brunette hair was sitting by herself, nervously clutching her purse in her lap. An idea bloomed in his mind, one that might be the answer to the problem of how to give Skylar back that "normal" life she wanted so badly.

He detoured to the woman. "Excuse me, are you Abigail Flores?"

"Yes, yes, I am. I'm here to see my employer, Mr. Scott. Are you his doctor?"

"No ma'am. My name is Adam Trent. I'm a friend of, ah, a mutual friend of ours. If you have a minute, I need to talk to you about that friend. I also have an urgent favor to ask you."

He motioned for the FBI agent to join them.

Chapter Twenty-Two

Skylar yawned and stretched the next morning as the sun's first rays slanted through the blinds on the window beside her hospital bed. The big round clock on the wall announced that it was a quarter till eight. She prayed it was the last eight o'clock in the morning she'd experience in this hospital. The doctors and staff had been wonderful. But lying in bed for so long was beyond boring.

A whisper of sound had her looking to her right. Poor Trent was sleeping in the extremely uncomfortable-looking visitor's chair. He'd come in and out many times to check on her. But the nurse kept telling him to let her sleep and they'd never gotten a chance to really talk. Judging by how wrinkled his suit was, he must have slept in it.

Her heart swelled as she watched him. Never in her life had she known a man like him. Smart, brave, loyal, great in a gunfight, and gorgeous to a fault. And he cared about her. Just knowing that had crazy hopes swirling through her mind. Hopes for a future, a normal life, with him. But it would only be a dream if there wasn't some way to ensure that she'd be safe from the Lancasters.

Living in fear was no way to live. She wouldn't wish it on anyone. And even though it would break her heart to never see him again, that's what she'd do if it meant letting *him* live a normal life. He deserved so much more than to be tied to a woman who was always looking over her shoulder.

He stirred in his chair, blinking and sitting up. When he saw her watching him, he gave her a sleepy smile. "Morning."

"Morning. You didn't need to stay here all night. I would have been fine."

He glanced at the clock, then straightened. "Almost eight. Good grief. I didn't mean to fall asleep. Thankfully, Callum's guarding your room. Anyone could have come in otherwise." He shook his head, obviously disgusted with himself.

"Guarding my room? You really think Scott's men would try something in a hospital?"

"I think until that deadline passes, anything's possible. But I may have a solution to our problems. Give me a minute. I'll explain, but my bladder is about to burst."

She laughed as he jogged around the bed and headed into the connected bathroom. When he came out, he gave her a sheepish grin. "I stole some of your toothpaste. Don't worry. I used my finger, not your toothbrush."

"Well, thank goodness," she teased. "But in payment for my pilfered toothpaste, you have to lower this stupid railing. You're not the only one who needs to hurry to the bathroom."

"Your wish is my command." He lowered the railing and offered his hand to help her.

She almost refused, feeling silly since there wasn't anything wrong with her. But lying in bed had made her wobbly on her feet and unexpectedly dizzy. She might have fallen if he hadn't been holding her up.

After seeing to her needs—including the toothbrush—she climbed back in bed, with his help.

"Stop looking so worried," she told him. "I'm fine."

He didn't seem convinced as he clicked the railing into place. But he didn't argue. He returned to his chair on the other side of the bed. "I want you to listen to this recording." He thumbed through some screens on his phone.

"A recording of what?"

He set the phone on the bed beside her. "Scott and Phoebe Lancaster talking in his hospital room yesterday afternoon."

He pressed the screen, then sat with his forearms resting on the railing.

Skylar sat in shock as the conversation played. Even though Scott's voice was gravelly and rough from having been punched in the throat, his words came through clearly. He and Phoebe talked openly about the will's upcoming five-year deadline and that they still needed to kill Skylar. They discussed the worst-case scenario, that if she wasn't dead by then and went to the trustees, they'd have to bribe or potentially kill the trustees, or figure out some other way to prevent her from inheriting. Nothing was going to stand in their way of the money they felt they deserved.

She shook her head in disgust, her stomach twisting

at the thought that she was actually related to these horrible people. Then it got worse. Phoebe complained that when Scott and Richard had killed Capone, they should have killed Mattly. Otherwise, all these years later the investigator—she assumed they meant Trent—wouldn't have talked to Mattly and gotten curious about the will.

They argued, each of them angry and nasty with each other. She blamed him for everything that had gone wrong and he blamed her.

"It would have looked too suspicious killing both lawyers at the same time," he insisted. "I kept tabs on Mattly over the years to see if he knew anything about the bookie and loan shark businesses that we forced Capone to help us run. Never seemed as if he knew anything except about our legit enterprises. With the deadline growing closer, I kept more frequent tabs on him, just in case he knew more than I thought he did. You should be thanking me for that. Otherwise, we wouldn't have known that the Skylar witch was in town and we wouldn't have figured out about the rental house."

"If you'd taken care of Mattly years ago—and Skylar—Richard would still be alive."

They devolved into more heated arguments. Trent turned off the recording.

Skylar sat there, stunned. "What vicious, nasty, horrible people."

"The worst. I was pleasantly surprised they spoke so openly, as was the FBI agent who helped me set this up. I guess with Richard dead and Scott hurt, they both were emotional and sloppy. Lucky for us, we were able to take advantage of it."

"How? I can't imagine them talking like that with anyone else in the room."

"They didn't. I convinced one of Scott's visitors to plant a tiny recording device, a bug, on Scott's bedframe. The FBI got a warrant to plant it based on statements from that same visitor, information they knew about Scott and Phoebe Lancaster's criminal activities from overhearing conversations over the years. You only heard a small part of the conversation. They went on to discuss strategies for keeping their illegal businesses going. Apparently Richard was the brainchild behind everything and they're worried about how to keep operating without him."

"I'm afraid to hope. But this is good news for me, right?"

"The best. They admitted to murder and a dozen federal crimes. The FBI got a search warrant based on the recording and is at the mansion right now. They already texted me that there's a gold mine of evidence there. They'll both be going to prison for a very long time. You're free, Skylar. You can live your life without looking over your shoulder anymore."

She burst into tears.

He lowered the railing and climbed into the bed beside her. She clung to him as he rocked her and stroked her hair.

A knock sounded on the door and Callum stepped in. His brows arched in surprise when he saw them.

"Yes?" Trent's voice was short, unapologetic.

"Right, um, you told someone to meet you here around eight. They've been waiting in the hallway for several minutes. Do you want me to tell them to come back later?"

Trent glanced at the clock. Five after eight. He swore.

Skylar pulled back and wiped her eyes. "I'm sorry. You have a meeting? It's okay to leave. I'll be fine, really." She sniffed and wiped her eyes again.

He kissed her forehead and climbed out of the bed. After raising the railing, he looked at Callum, who was watching them with undisguised interest. "Give us one minute. Then send them in."

"Will do." He stepped outside and closed the door.

"Skylar, I asked someone to meet *you* here, not me. It's the person who gave the FBI the information they needed to get that search warrant for the mansion. And the person who was brave enough to place the bug in Scott's hospital room. I thought you might want to meet them."

She wiped her face and fluffed her hair as she scooted farther up in the bed. "Of course. So many people have helped me. Especially you. I'd love the opportunity to thank one of them."

Before Trent could finish explaining about the visitor, Callum opened the door and ushered her inside.

There was no point in a further delay now. He motioned toward the woman. "Skylar, meet your maternal grandmother, Abigail Flores."

Abigail ran to Skylar's bed. They collapsed in tears as they wrapped their arms around each other.

Chapter Twenty-Three

Trent sat on the aisle side of the courtroom bench a few rows behind the prosecution table, blocking anyone else from getting near Skylar beside him. If they wanted to watch the hearing, they could find another bench.

Phoebe and Scott Lancaster were far too close to Skylar for his comfort. Even though they were wearing shackles at the defense table, he didn't like such evil being in the same room as the woman he cared about.

"Stop glaring at them," Skylar whispered. "You're worrying the bailiff. He keeps watching you as if he thinks you're going to run over there and hurt the Lancasters."

She was right. The bailiff was watching him and looked nervous. Smart man. Trent very much wanted to break Scott's neck. But there were too many deputies in the courtroom. It wasn't worth being arrested for the small amount of damage he'd be able to do before being tackled. Then again. Another solid punch to Scott's throat might finish what he'd started in the woods. That might be worth going to jail.

"Trent," she whispered again. "Seriously. Stop."

He sighed. "I'll be good. But I still don't understand

why you insisted on coming here. You've only been out of the hospital for a day."

"Whose fault is that?" she grumbled. "I'd have been out a week ago if you hadn't told the doctor about that dizzy spell and the inconsequential headache that began after Abigail left."

"You suffered a serious blow to your head. And that inconsequential headache was a debilitating migraine, on top of the dizzy spell. I won't apologize for being concerned and telling your neurologist. Blame him for keeping you there a whole week. He's the one who kept running tests."

"Tests that proved the only thing wrong with me was stress. How humiliating is that?"

"It's completely understandable. Which begs the question, again, why do you feel it's so important to sit through this bail hearing? There's no way the judge is going to let them out of jail. The FBI found enough evidence in the mansion to put both of them away for life. There won't be any early releases either. Federal prisons don't have parole."

"I'm not worried about them. I'm worried about Phoebe's son, Randolph. I was hoping he'd show up today so I can talk to him."

"He doesn't want to talk to you. He refused all of your requests via his court-appointed guardian. Besides, do you even know what he looks like?"

"Abigail showed me pictures on her phone. I just want to talk to him for a few minutes. He needs to know he's not alone, that we're both Martha's grandchildren and should be there for each other. I don't want him growing up blaming me for what happened to his family; maybe even hating me."

"Give him some time. Once he matures, maybe he'll be willing to talk to you."

"He turns eighteen next month. What will happen to him then? He won't have a guardian anymore to guide him. He'll be all alone."

"Even with the judge freezing the bulk of Martha's estate while the Feds sort out legally gained money from illegally gained money, the judge made sure that Randolph has a generous allowance. He'll have everything he needs. Still, if it's bothering you, I'll see what I can do to get him to agree to a meeting. But there's no way you'll meet with him alone. I'll be there with you."

She gave him a searching look. "You don't think he'll become a threat to me like his parents, do you?"

"Doubtful. Right now his guardian is charged with both taking care of him and making sure he doesn't get into trouble. After his eighteenth birthday, when the guardian leaves, he knows the FBI, the police and a security team I'll hire will keep tabs on him. If he even jaywalks, I'll make sure his butt is thrown in jail."

She rolled her eyes. "That's not the type of guidance I had in mind. He needs love and understanding. I know what it's like to lose your parents. He's lost his at a very young age. Losing his mom to prison has to feel ten times worse."

The bailiff instructed everyone to rise for the judge.

Skylar scanned the audience again as they stood.

"He's not coming," Trent whispered.

She sighed.

As Trent had predicted, no bail was granted. Scott

and Phoebe Lancaster were led away in chains to spend the rest of their lives locked up—in jail for now. After their trials, they'd be moved to a maximum security federal prison. Finally, Skylar was truly safe.

He ushered her down the front steps outside the courthouse. Callum met them on the sidewalk and hugged Skylar.

"Congratulations," he told her. "It's finally officially over."

She smiled. "I guess it is. Thanks for being here with us. It was nice of you to drive all the way to Chattanooga for a thirty-minute hearing, even though you didn't get to sit in on it."

"I didn't expect to. After all, who else would hold onto Trent's gun while he was in the courthouse?" He laughed and handed the pistol to Trent. "I know you feel naked without this. 'Always packing' is your motto."

"One of many," Skylar teased.

"Thanks, Callum. It did feel weird sitting in the same room with the Lancasters without being armed."

"Courthouse security knows better than to let the families of victims carry weapons inside," Callum said. "That's a recipe for disaster."

"Survivor," Skylar corrected. "Not victim."

"My bad." Callum smiled.

"I know a great place here in the downtown area for lunch," Trent said, as they headed toward his SUV—the new one he'd bought a few days ago since the old one had bullet holes all through it.

"You're not the only one who knows some great restaurants around here," she said. "I used to live here too, you know."

He turned to answer a question Callum asked him.

"Randolph, don't!" Skylar screamed.

Callum and Trent whirled around, bringing up their pistols lightning fast. Randolph was pointing a gun at them from across the street.

"No, don't!" Skylar jumped forward, grabbing for Trent's arm.

Bam! Bam! Bam!

Randolph crumpled to the sidewalk.

Trent whirled around to check on Skylar. She was on her back, eyes closed, blood seeping around her on the concrete. Cold terror congealed in his chest as he dropped to his knees beside her. There was a bullet hole in her shirt.

"She's been hit! Callum, call 911. Skylar, Skylar, hold on, sweetheart. Hold on."

Chapter Twenty-Four

Skylar adjusted the bouquet of red roses on Randolph's grave one last time, then straightened and looked out at the rolling fields around her. Acres of land surrounded by pristine white three-rail fencing marked it as Lancaster territory. And the gorgeous Thoroughbreds curiously watching her from behind one of those fences made her smile.

Phoebe had requested that Randolph be buried here, on the horse ranch where he'd grown up. Since the judge had given ownership of the mansion and all of this land to Skylar, it had been her duty to respond. Of course, she'd told her yes, and oversaw the arrangements.

The Feds wouldn't let Phoebe out of prison for the funeral. So Skylar had seen to that as well, holding a wake yesterday at the mansion for his school friends and the household staff who'd known him since he was born. Her grandmother had been there too, helping her with everything. And she was going to send pictures of the grave and flowers to Phoebe to take that burden off Skylar.

Signing over the deed on the mansion and this property to her grandmother had taken another burden away.

She wanted nothing to do with this place, as beautiful as it was. But it had been her grandmother's home away from home for decades. She'd cried happy tears when Skylar gave her the paperwork, along with a healthy bank account to ensure she'd never have to work again. At least that was one good thing to come out of all this.

Since her grandmother lived here now, Skylar would come back to visit on occasion. But she had no desire to stay. Her home was somewhere else entirely. And it had taken her far too long to figure that out.

She headed down the hill toward the four-wheeler she'd borrowed to get up here. Although, technically, she guessed she owned it now. Or, rather, her grandmother did. Everything was so strange. Her world had completely changed. Some of it for the better, some of it not. Learning she was a Lancaster wasn't one of the good things. But learning she had a loving, wonderful grandmother definitely was.

After passing through the open gate, she jumped off the four-wheeler and closed it behind her. She turned around and her heart leaped in her chest when she saw a man leaning against a tree a few yards away. Relief flooded through her a split second later when she realized it was Trent.

She self-consciously smoothed her jeans and then patted her hair, which was still much shorter than she was used to. "How did you find me?"

"I'm a detective. I like your hair. Back to your natural color. Black suits you."

"It's dark brown. But thanks."

"Why have you been hiding from me and avoiding my calls since getting out of the hospital?"

She leaned against the fence. "I haven't been hiding. I've been…thinking. I needed some time to figure things out."

"You're never going to forgive me for killing Randolph, are you? That compass hanging on the chain around your neck is proof enough that he was deadly serious about killing you. If it hadn't stopped that bullet, you'd be dead instead of recovering from a concussion and having stitches in the back of your head."

"He wasn't shooting at me. He was shooting at you."

He stared at her a long moment, then swore. "You jumped in front of me to take that bullet, didn't you?"

"I jumped in front of you to stop you from shooting Randolph."

"You could have been killed trying to save someone not worth saving."

She gasped. "How can you say that? He was a child."

"That so-called child murdered his guardian so he could get out of the house and come after us at the courthouse."

She shivered. "I know. I know. I'm trying to come to grips with all of it. Like I said, I needed time to think." She pulled the necklace out from beneath her shirt and ran a finger across the bullet embedded in the front of the compass.

"I can't believe you're still wearing that. Why do you want a continual reminder of someone almost killing you?"

She dropped the necklace back beneath her shirt and met his gaze. "It's not a reminder about Randolph. It's a reminder about my dad. He spent his whole life trying to save me. If it wasn't for his training, I'd have been dead long ago. And in the end, giving me that compass was like him reaching out from the grave one more time to save my life, and point me in a new direction."

She took a step toward him, then another until they were almost touching.

"He saved my life by saving yours." She gently smoothed her fingers across his cheeks. "If I hadn't jumped in front of you, that bullet would have ended up in your chest, not my necklace."

He swore again. "I knew you were sacrificing yourself for me."

"I'm more selfish than that. I'd hoped to save my cousin *and* you. If you'd been killed, I'd have died too, just the same as if that bullet had pierced my own heart. I don't blame you for anything, Trent. I blame myself for almost losing you. I should have listened to your warnings. I shouldn't have gone to that hearing. It almost cost me the most precious thing I've ever found. You."

His hands shook as he grasped her shoulders. "What are you saying, Skylar? You haven't spoken to me in over a week and I've assumed the worst. So I need you to make it very clear."

"I love you. How's that for clarity?"

His beautiful blue eyes widened in surprise. Suddenly, she was in his arms and he was twirling her around, laughing and planting kisses all across her face.

She laughed until her sides hurt. "Stop, stop, I'm getting dizzy."

He immediately stopped and looked down at her, his brow furrowed with concern. "Are you okay? I shouldn't have done that. That was stupid of me. Does your head hurt? Are you still dizzy—"

She laughed and pressed her hand over his mouth. "Stop worrying so much. I'm fine. Anyone would be dizzy being swung around like that. You can put me down now, though."

He gently lowered her until she was standing and held on to her waist to steady her.

"You don't have to be so gentle. I'm not fragile."

"Maybe not. But you *are* precious. I don't ever want anything to happen to you. I lost someone I loved dearly, still love, and I don't think I could survive something like that again."

Her heart nearly broke at his words. "Your wife? Tanya?"

He nodded. "Sorry. I shouldn't have mentioned her, even indirectly."

"Of course you should have. She's a part of you. We should never forget the ones we love who've passed on. We should carry them in our hearts forever."

"You're an amazing woman, Skylar Lancaster."

She grimaced. "I hate that name."

"Maybe we should change it one more time. I was thinking Skylar Trent has a nice ring to it."

She stared up at him in wonder. "Is there a question buried in there somewhere, Adam Trent?"

He grinned. "I love you, Skylar. With all my heart and soul. Will you do me the honor of becoming my wife?"

"Took you long enough to get around to that. And if you can't figure it out, the answer is yes."

He was laughing when he kissed her.

When they finally came up for air, he smiled. "You have enough money to live anywhere in the world now. Where do you want to call home?"

"Home isn't a place. It's a feeling. My home is wherever you are." She gently pressed another kiss against his lips. "Take me home, Trent."

And so he did.

* * * * *

Look for the next book in Lena Diaz's miniseries,
A Tennessee Cold Case Story, *coming soon!*

And in case you missed them, check out the first two titles in the series:

Murder on Prescott Mountain
Serial Slayer Cold Case

You'll find them wherever Harlequin Intrigue books are sold!

COMING NEXT MONTH FROM

HARLEQUIN

INTRIGUE

#2163 LAST SEEN IN SILVER CREEK

Silver Creek Lawmen: Second Generation • by Delores Fossen

As the new sheriff of Silver Creek, Theo Sheldon must face down the killer who murdered his parents while protecting the killer's new target, Kim Ryland. Kim and Theo have spent years resisting one another, but now they must join forces to stay alive.

#2164 DECEPTION AT DIXON PASS

Eagle Mountain: Critical Response • by Cindi Myers

US Marshall Declan Owen has no memory of his identity—nor of the murder he's been accused of committing. Scientist Grace Wilcox agrees to help him uncover the truth. But their investigation turns deadly when the real culprit places the reluctant duo in their crosshairs.

#2165 CLANDESTINE BABY

Covert Cowboy Soldiers • by Nicole Helm

When Cal Thompson finds a bloody, unconscious woman near his ranch, he's more surprised by her identity...and the little bundle she carries. Norah Young doesn't remember anything—including the name of the baby she fought to save. And all Cal knows is she's the wife he had been told was dead...

#2166 WYOMING COWBOY UNDERCOVER

Cowboy State Lawmen • by Juno Rushdan

ATF Agent Rocco Sharp must infiltrate a cult to expose an illegal weapons supplier. But getting up close and personal with Mercy McCoy, the leader's daughter, raises the stakes considerably. When a bombing plot is discovered and Rocco's cover is compromised, Mercy will choose between family loyalty and love.

#2167 TEXAS BODYGUARD: CHANCE

San Antonio Security • by Janie Crouch

Security specialist Chance Patterson has a reputation for safeguarding his charges. But Maci Ford isn't *technically* his charge. She's the doppelgänger decoy to catch a stalker. But trusting Maci could be even more precarious. She's keeping secrets...and being pregnant with Chance's baby is just the beginning...

#2168 HIGH MOUNTAIN TERROR

by Janice Kay Johnson

When a wilderness photography excursion leads Ava Brevik to terrorist arms dealers, detective Zach Reeves risks everything to protect her. But navigating remote, snow-clad mountains together with no contact with the outside world threatens every survival skill—and romantic safeguard—they've got.